READ-ALOUD POEMS
FOR YOUNG PEOPLE

READ-ALOUD POEMS FOR YOUNG PEOPLE

AN INTRODUCTION TO THE MAGIC AND EXCITEMENT OF POETRY

Edited by Glorya Hale

BLACK DOG
& LEVENTHAL
PUBLISHERS
NEW YORK

In memory of E.L.R.
and for Dylan, his first great grandchild

Published by
Black Dog & Leventhal Publishers, Inc.
151 West 19th Street, New York, NY 10011

Distributed by
Workman Publishing Company
708 Broadway, New York, NY 10003

Book Design by Liz Trovato

Manufactured in the United States of America

ISBN: 1-884822-99-1
Soft cover edition ISBN: 1–57912–051–2

j i h g f e d c

Library of Congress Cataloging-in-Publication Data
Read-aloud poems for young people: selections from the world's best-loved
verses / edited by Glorya Hale.
p.   cm.
Includes index of authors.
Summary : A collection of verses in such catagories as "Meet the Family,"
"Love and Country," "Poems That Tell Stroies," and "Special Places."
ISBN 1-884822-99-1 (alk. paper)
1. Children's poetry, English.   2. Children's poetry, American.
3. Oral interpretation of poetry—Juvenile literature.
[1. Poetry--Collections.] I. Hale, Glorya.
PR1175.3.R425 1997
821.008'09282—dc21   97-37235
                                                         CIP
                                                         AC

CONTENTS

MEET THE FAMILY   59

JUST ME 101

POEMS THAT TELL STORIES

INTRODUCTION

I have cherished childhood memories of listening to my father read poetry to me. He had a deep, melodious voice and read slowly, with great expression. Many of the poems he chose were written for "grownups" and often, before reading one of these, he would tell me something about the poet or about the poem itself. He made me aware of the magic, the beauty, and the fun of poetry. He gave it an immediacy. Most of all, he conveyed his own love of poetry.

When he read "Hiawatha" we both marveled at the way Longfellow had captured the rhythm of the Indian tom toms. We wondered if "The Raven" would have been so dramatic a poem if instead of a raven the bird sitting above the chamber door had been an owl, as Edgar Allan Poe originally intended. He recited John Milton's "Sonnet on His Blindness" and we imagined what it would be like to lose our sight. I would giggle all through Lewis Carroll's "Jabberwocky," which he read quite seriously, as if the words made perfect sense. And even as a little girl I was enchanted by the love story of Elizabeth Barrett and Robert Browning and as I listened to her sonnet "How do I love thee?" I realized, although not in these words, that poetry gives voice to emotions.

It has, therefore, been with the greatest pleasure and care that I have chosen the poems for this book. Included are the classic poems that I loved as a child, poems that I memorized then, and can still recite. There are also contemporary poems that I discovered later, with my own children and in the course of my own reading as an adult. Some of the poems have been included at the suggestion of teachers and of young friends. Many of the poems are annotated with short biographies of the poets, amusing stories about the poems, or information about the circumstances in which they were written.

The poems in this collection have been organized by subject, rather than chronologically or alphabetically by author, thus making them more accessible to the browser searching for a favorite poem or one suited to the mood of the moment. There are poems that tell stories written by such fine storytellers as Henry Wadsworth Longfellow, Edgar Allan Poe, and William Butler Yeats; poems that are guaranteed to make even the most serious person laugh, since they are the work of such amazing versifiers as Shel Silverstein, Ogden Nash, Lewis Carroll, and Edward Lear; and poems about friendship and love by such great writers as Robert Frost, William Blake, and Elizabeth Barrett Browning.

Robert Graves, W. H. Auden, E. E. Cummings, and J.R.R. Tolkien are among those who create a make-believe land of Let's Pretend which is, of course, inhabited by fairies and goblins, giants and witches. A hippopotamus and an elephant, a chipmunk and a dog, butterflies and fireflies, a camel and a sloth, are some of Nature's People who poets like Theodore Roethke, Randall Jarrell, Emily Dickinson, Jack Prelutsky, and Ted Hughes describe. In the section Meet the Family, Langston Hughes remembers "Aunt Sue's Stories," Alfred Noyes tells about the day when "Daddy Fell Into the Pond," Michael Ondaatje writes "To a Sad Daughter," and Judith Viorst explains why "Mother Doesn't Want a Dog."

In Just Me, Edna St. Vincent Millay, Maya Angelou, Noel Coward, and May Swenson describe their own feelings when they were young. Vachel Lindsay, Elias Lieberman, Walt Whitman, and Robert Browning are some of the poets who write about Love of Country; Elinor Wylie, Sara Teasdale, Carl Sandburg, and Seamus Heaney are among those represented in Poetry of the Earth—and the Sky. Dylan Thomas, William Wordsworth, and Countee Cullen write about Special Places. Poems to Ponder includes works by Amy Lowell, John Keats, T.S. Eliot, John Milton, and Richard Wilbur.

The intention of this book is to introduce young people to the magic and the excitement of poetry. But when an adult reads poems aloud to the special child in his or her life they share a valuable experience that they will both treasure.

GLORYA HALE

NATURE'S PEOPLE

❧ In Emily Dickenson's poem "The Snake," she refers to "nature's people." In this section you will make the acquaintance of many of nature's people including kittens and dogs, a sloth and a camel, a tiger and a crocodile, and, of course, Emily Dickenson's snake.

CHOOSING THEIR NAMES

Our old cat has kittens three—
What do you think their names should be?
One is tabby with emerald eyes,
    And a tail that's long and slender,
And into a temper she quickly flies
    If you ever by chance offend her.
    I think we shall call her this—
        I think we shall call her that—
Now, don't you think that Pepperpot
    Is a nice name for a cat?

One is black with a frill of white,
    And her feet are all white fur,
If you stroke her she carries her tail upright
    And quickly begins to purr.
    I think we shall call her this—
        I think we shall call her that—
Now, don't you think that Sootikin
    Is a nice name for a cat?

One is a tortoiseshell yellow and black,
    With plenty of white about him;
If you tease him, at once he sets up his back,
    He's a quarrelsome one, ne'er doubt him.
    I think we shall call him this—
        I think we shall call him that—
Now, don't you think that Scratchaway
    Is a nice name for a cat?

Our old cat has kittens three
And I fancy these their names will be:
Pepperpot, Sootikin, Scratchaway—there!
Were ever kittens with these to compare?
And we call the old mother—
    Now, what do you think?
Tabitha Longclaws Tiddley Wink.

THOMAS HOOD

THE KITTEN AT PLAY

See the kitten on the wall,
Sporting with the leaves that fall,
Withered leaves, one, two, and three
Falling from the elder tree,
Through the calm and frosty air
Of the morning bright and fair.

See the kitten, how she starts,
Crouches, stretches, paws, and darts
With a tiger-leap half way
Now she meets her coming prey.
Lets it go as fast and then
Has it in her power again.

Now she works with three and four,
Like an Indian conjurer;
Quick as he in feats of art,
Gracefully she plays her part;
Yet were gazing thousands there,
What would little Tabby care?

WILLIAM WORDSWORTH

THAT CAT

The cat that comes to my window sill
When the moon looks cold and the night is still—
He comes in a frenzied state alone
With a tail that stands like a pine tree cone,
And says: "I have finished my evening lark,
And I think I can hear a hound dog bark.
My whiskers are froze 'nd stuck to my chin.
I do wish you'd git up and let me in."
      That cat gits in.

But if in the solitude of the night
He doesn't appear to be feeling right,
And rises and stretches and seeks the floor,
And some remote corner he would explore,
And doesn't feel satisfied just because
There's no good spot for to sharpen his claws,
And meows and canters uneasy about
Beyond the least shadow of any doubt
      That cat gits out.

BEN KING

ROGER THE DOG

Asleep he wheezes at his ease.
He only wakes to scratch his fleas.

He hogs the fire, he bakes his head
As if it were a loaf of bread.

He's just a sack of snoring dog,
You can lug him like a log.

You can roll him with your foot,
He'll stay snoring where he's put.

I take him out for exercise,
He rolls in cowclap up to his eyes.

He will not race, he will not romp,
He saves his strength for boggle and chomp.

He'll work as hard as you could wish
Emptying his dinner dish,

Then flops flat, and digs down deep,
Like a miner, into sleep.

TED HUGHES

LONE DOG

I'm a lean dog, a keen dog, a wild dog, and lone;
I'm a rough dog, a tough dog, hunting on my own;
I'm a bad dog, a mad dog, teasing silly sheep;
I love to sit and bay the moon, to keep fat souls from sleep.

I'll never be a lap dog, licking dirty feet,
A sleek dog, a meek dog, cringing for my meat,
Not for me the fireside, the well-filled plate,
But shut door, and sharp stone, and cuff and kick and hate.

Not for me the other dogs, running by my side,
Some have run a short while, but none of them would bide,
Oh, mine is still the lone trail, the hard trail, the best,
Wide wind, and wild stars, and hunger of the quest!

IRENE RUTHERFORD MCLEOD

THE COW

The friendly cow all red and white,
    I love with all my heart:
She gives me cream with all her might,
    To eat with apple tart.

She wanders lowing here and there,
    And yet she cannot stray,
All in the pleasant open air,
    The pleasant light of day;

And blown by all the winds that pass
    And wet with all the showers,
She walks among the meadow grass
    And eats the meadow flowers.

ROBERT LOUIS STEVENSON

Many of Robert Louis Stevenson's poems are included in this book. Most of them come from his collection of poems—A Child's Garden of Verses. Stevenson also wrote travel books and such famous novels as Treasure Island and Dr. Jekyll and Mr. Hyde.

THE DONKEY

I saw a donkey
One day old,
His head was too big
For his neck to hold;
His legs were shaky
And long and loose,
They rocked and staggered
And weren't much use.
He tried to gambol
And frisk a bit,
But he wasn't quite sure
Of the trick of it.
His queer little coat
Was soft and gray
And curled at his neck
In a lovely way.
His face was wistful
And left no doubt
That he felt life needed
Some thinking about.
So he blundered round
In venturesome quest,
And then lay flat
On the ground to rest.
He looked so little
And weak and slim,
I prayed the world
Might be good to him.

AUTHOR UNKNOWN

THE TIGER

Tiger! Tiger! burning bright,
In the forests of the night,
What immortal hand or eye
Could frame thy fearful symmetry?

In what distant deeps or skies
Burnt the fire of thine eyes?
On what wings dare he aspire?
What the hand dare seize the fire?

And what shoulder, and what art,
Could twist the sinews of thy heart?
And when thy heart began to beat,
What dread hand and what dread feet?

What the hammer? what the chain?
In what furnace was thy brain?
What the anvil? what dread grasp
Dare its deadly terrors clasp?

When the stars threw down their spears,
And watered heaven with their tears,
Did He smile His work to see?
Did He who made the Lamb, make thee?

Tiger! Tiger! burning bright,
In the forests of the night,
What immortal hand or eye
Dare frame thy fearful symmetry?

WILLIAM BLAKE

William Blake was born in London in 1757 and lived there all his life. In addition to being a poet, he was an artist and an engraver. This poem was included in his book Songs of Experience; *it was hand-lettered and illustrated with Blake's drawing of a tiger prowling through the jungle.*

⌒ *Bret Harte, who was born in Albany, New York, was eighteen years old when he went to California where he worked as a gold-miner, a school teacher, a Wells Fargo expressman, and a printer and a journalist. He is most famous today for his stories of Western life.*

GRIZZLY

Coward—of heroic size,
In whose lazy muscles lies
Strength we fear and yet despise;
Savage—whose relentless tusks
Are content with acorn husks;
Robber—whose exploits ne'er soared
O'er the bee's or squirrel's hoard;
Whiskered chin and feeble nose,
Claws of steel on baby toes,
Here, in solitude and shade,
Shambling, shuffling plantigrade,
Be thy courses undismayed!
Here, where Nature makes thy bed,
Let thy rude, half-human tread
    Point to hidden Indian springs,
Lost in ferns and fragrant grasses,
    Hovered o'er by timid wings,
Where the wood duck lightly passes,
Where the wild bee holds her sweets—
Epicurean retreats,
Fit for thee, and better than
Fearful spoils of dangerous man.
In thy fat-jowled deviltry
Friar Tuck shall live in thee;
Thou mayst levy tithe and dole;
    Thou shalt spread the woodland cheer,
From the pilgrim taking toll;
    Match thy cunning with his fear;
Eat, and drink, and have thy fill;
Yet remain an outlaw still!

BRET HARTE

THE LION

When Lion sends his roaring forth,
Silence falls upon the earth;
For the creatures, great and small,
Know his terror-breathing call;
And, as if by death pursued,
Leave him to a solitude.

Lion, thou art made to dwell
In hot lands, intractable,
And thyself, the sun, the sand,
Are a tyrannous triple band;
Lion-king and desert throne,
All the region is your own!

MARY HOWETT

THE LION

The lion, the lion, he dwells in the waste,
He has a big head and a very small waist;
But his shoulders are stark,
And his jaws they are grim,
And a good little child will not play with him.

HILAIRE BELLOC

THE CAMEL'S COMPLAINT

Canary birds feed on sugar and seed,
    Parrots have crackers to crunch;
And as for the poodles, they tell me the noodles
    Have chicken and cream for their lunch.
        But there's never a question
        About my digestion—
            Anything does for me.

Cats, you're aware, can repose in a chair,
    Chickens can roost upon rails;
Puppies are able to sleep in a stable,
    And oysters can slumber in pails.
        But no one supposes
        A poor camel dozes—
            Any place does for me.

Lambs are enclosed where it's never exposed,
    Coops are constructed for hens;
Kittens are treated to houses well heated,
    And pigs are protected by pens.
        But a camel comes handy
        Wherever it's sandy—
            Anywhere does for me.

People would laugh if you rode a giraffe,
    Or mounted the back of an ox;
It's nobody's habit to ride on a rabbit,
    Or try to bestraddle a fox.
        But as for a camel, he's
        Ridden by families—
            Any load does for me.

Charles E. Carryl, an American, was a member of the New York Stock exchange. He wrote novels for children, which appeared in installments in the magazine St. Nicholas. Frequently, his prose was peppered with amusing verse, like this poem about the camel.

A snake is as round as a hole in the ground,
    And weasels are wavy and sleek;
And no alligator could ever be straighter
    Than lizards that live in a creek.
      But a camel's all lumpy
      And bumpy and humpy—
        Any shape does for me.

CHARLES E. CARRYL

THE HIPPOPOTAMUS

The huge hippopotamus hasn't a hair
on the back of his wrinkly hide;
he carries the bulk of his prominent hulk
rather loosely assembled inside.

The huge hippopotamus lives without care
at a slow philosophical pace,
as he wades in the mud with a thump and a thud
and a permanent grin on his face.

JACK PRELUTSKY

Jack Prelutsky, who was born in New York, has written many poems for children. The author of more than thirty poetry collections, he visits school and libraries all over the country where he reads to children.

THE BLIND MEN
AND THE ELEPHANT

It was six men of Indostan
    To learning much inclined,
Who went to see the elephant
    (Though all of them were blind),
That each by observation
    Might satisfy his mind.

The First approached the elephant,
    And, happening to fall
Against his broad and sturdy side,
    At once began to bawl:
"God bless me! but the elephant
    Is nothing but a wall!

The Second, feeling of the tusk,
    Cried: "Ho! What have we here
So very round and smooth and sharp?
    To me 'tis mighty clear
This wonder of an elephant
    Is very like a spear!"

The Third approached the animal
    And, happening to take
The squirming trunk within his hands,
    Thus boldly up and spake:
"I see," quoth he, "the elephant
    Is very like a snake!"

Born and educated in Vermont, John Godfrey Saxe was a lawyer and a journalist. He was editor of the Burlington, Vermont, Sentinel, served as the state's attorney general, and ran, unsuccessfully, for governor. His books of humorous verse were popular in their day, but now only this poem is remembered.

The Fourth reached out his eager hand,
    And felt about the knee:
"What most this wondrous beast is like
    Is mighty plain," quoth he;
" 'Tis clear enough the elephant
    Is very like a tree."

The Fifth, who chanced to touch the ear,
    Said: "E'en the blindest man
Can tell what this resembles most;
    Deny the fact who can,
This marvel of an elephant
    Is very like a fan!"

The Sixth no sooner had begun
    About the beast to grope,
Than, seizing on the swinging tail
    That fell within his scope,
"I see," quoth he, "the elephant
    Is very like a rope!"

And so these men of Indostan
    Disputed loud and long,
Each in his own opinion
    Exceeding stiff and strong,
Though each was partly in the right,
    And all were in the wrong!

So, oft in theologic wars
    The disputants, I ween,
Rail on in utter ignorance
    Of what each other mean,
And prate about an elephant
    Not one of them has seen!

JOHN GODFREY SAXE

Theodore Roethke is one of America's most respected modern poets. Born in Michigan, he spent much of his adult life in the northwest, teaching at the University of Washington. He won many awards, including the Pulitzer Prize in 1953 and a National Book Award in 1965. His poems, some of which were written for children, demonstrate both the serious and, as in this one, the comic sides of his temperament.

THE SLOTH

In moving-slow he has no Peer.
You ask him something in his ear;
He thinks about it for a Year;

And, then, before he says a Word
There, upside down (unlike a Bird)
He will assume that you have Heard—

A most Ex-as-per-at-ing Lug.
But should you call his manner Smug,
He'll sigh and give his Branch a Hug;

Then off to Sleep he goes,
Still swaying gently by his Toes,
And you just know he knows he knows.

THEODORE ROETHKE

THE CHIPMUNK'S DAY

In and out the bushes, up the ivy,
Into the hole
By the old oak stump, the chipmunk flashes.
Up the pole.

To the feeder full of seeds he dashes,
Stuffs his cheeks,
The chickadee and titmouse scold him,
Down he streaks.

Red as the leaves the wind blows off the maple,
Red as a fox,
Striped like a skunk, the chipmunk whistles
Past the love seat, past the mailbox,

Down the path,
Home to his warm hole stuffed with sweet
Things to eat.
Neat and slight and shining, his front feet

Curled at his breast, he sits there while the sun
Stripes the red west
With its last light: the chipmunk
Dives to his rest.

RANDALL JARRELL

Randall Jarrell, a leading American poet, critic, translator, and novelist, was born in Tennessee. He was a pilot in the Pacific during World War II.

BATS

A bat is born
Naked and blind and pale.
His mother makes a pocket of her tail
And catches him. He clings to her long fur
By his thumbs and toes and teeth.
And then the mother dances through the night
Doubling and looping, soaring, somersaulting—
Her baby hangs on underneath.

All night, in happiness, she hunts and flies.
Her high sharp cries
Like shining needlepoints of sound
Go out into the night and, echoing back,
Tell her what they have touched.
She hears how far it is, how big it is,
Which way it's going:
She lives by hearing.
The mother eats the moths and gnats she catches
In full flight; in full flight
The mother drinks the water of the pond
She skims across. Her baby hangs on tight.

Her baby drinks the milk she makes him
In moonlight or starlight, in mid-air.
Their single shadow, printed on the moon
Or fluttering across the stars,
Whirls on all night; at daybreak
The tired mother flaps home to her rafter.
The others all are there.

They hang themselves up by their toes,
They wrap themselves in their brown wings.
Bunched upside down, they sleep in air.
Their sharp ears, their sharp teeth, their quick sharp faces
Are dull and slow and mild.
All the bright day, as the mother sleeps,
She folds her wings about her sleeping child.

RANDALL JARRELL

MICE

I think mice
Are rather nice.

Their tails are long,
Their faces small,
They haven't any
Chins at all.
Their ears are pink,
Their teeth are white,
They run about
The house at night.
They nibble things
They shouldn't touch
And no one seems
To like them much.

But I think mice
Are nice.

ROSE FYLEMAN

THE HEN

The hen is a ferocious fowl,
She pecks you till she makes you howl.

And all the time she flaps her wings,
And says the most insulting things.

And when you try to take her eggs,
She bites large pieces from your legs.

The only safe way to get these,
Is to creep on your hands and knees.

In the meanwhile a friend must hide,
And jump out on the other side.

And then you snatch the eggs and run,
While she pursues the other one.

The difficulty is, to find
A trusty friend who will not mind.

LORD ALFRED DOUGLAS

TWO BIRDS AND THEIR NEST

Two guests from Alabama—two together,
And their nest, and four light-green eggs,
      spotted with brown,
And every day the he-bird, to and fro, near at hand,
And every day the she-bird, crouch'd on her nest,
      silent, with bright eyes,
And every day I, a curious boy, never too close,
      never disturbing them,
Cautiously peering.

WALT WHITMAN

Walt Whitman was born on Long Island, New York, in 1819, and grew up in Brooklyn. He worked as a printer, newspaperman, and schoolteacher. In 1855, he published the first edition of Leaves of Grass, *a book of highly original poetry which he enlarged throughout his life.*

⌒ *Although no one knows who wrote this poem, it is obvious that the phrase "beat upon the drum," in the last stanza, refers to the way the cuckoo changes its song from cuck oo, cuck oo, to cuck cuck, cuck cuck.*

THE CUCKOO IS A MERRY BIRD

The cuckoo is a merry bird,
She sings as she flies,
She brings us glad tidings
And tells us no lies.

She sucks the birds' eggs
To make her voice clear,
And the more she cries "Cuckoo"
The summer draws near.

The cuckoo is a lazy bird,
She never builds a nest,
She makes herself busy
By singing to the rest.

She never hatches her own young,
And that we all know,
And leaves it for some other bird
While she cries "Cuckoo."

And when her time is come
Her voice we no longer hear,
And where she goes we do not know
Until another year.

The cuckoo comes in April,
She sings a song in May,
In June she beats upon the drum,
And then she'll fly away.

AUTHOR UNKNOWN

PROUD SONGSTERS

The thrushes sing as the sun is going,
    And the finches whistle in ones and pairs,
And as it gets dark loud nightingales
    In bushes
Pipe, as they can when April wears,
    As if all Time were theirs.

These are brand new birds of twelve-months' growing
    Which a year ago, or less than twain
No finches were, nor nightingales,
    Nor thrushes,
But only particles of grain,
    And earth, and air, and rain.

THOMAS HARDY

Thomas Hardy was born in Dorset in England in 1840. Although he is best-known today as the author of such novels as Tess of the D'Urbervilles *and* The Return of the Native, *he always considered himself primarily a poet.*

⁓ *Celia Thaxter grew up on the Isles of Shoals, off the coast of New Hampshire, where her father was the lighthouse keeper. In the nineteenth century she was one of the best known women poets. She wrote for adults as well as for children. "The Sand-piper" is one of her most popular poems.*

THE SANDPIPER

Across the lonely beach we flit,
    One little sandpiper and I;
And fast I gather, bit by bit,
    The scattered driftwood, bleached and dry.
The wild waves reach their hands for it,
    The wild wind raves, the tide runs high,
As up and down the beach we flit—
    One little sandpiper and I.

Above our heads the sullen clouds
    Scud black and swift across the sky;
Like silent ghosts in misty shrouds
    Stand out the white lighthouses high.
Almost as far as eye can reach
    I see the close-reefed vessels fly,
As fast we flit along the beach—
    One little sandpiper and I.

I watch him as he skims along
    Uttering his sweet and mournful cry;
He starts not at my fitful song
    Or flash of fluttering drapery.
He has no thought of any wrong,
    He scans me with a fearless eye;
Staunch friends are we, well-tried and strong,
    The little sandpiper and I.

Comrade, where wilt thou be tonight
    When the loosed storm breaks furiously?
My driftwood fire will burn so bright!
    To what warm shelter canst thou fly?
I do not feel for thee, though wroth
    The tempest rushes through the sky:
For are we not God's children both,
    Thou, little sandpiper, and I?

CELIA THAXTER

THE ROBIN

The robin is the one
That interrupts the morn
With hurried, few, express reports
When March is scarcely on.

The robin is the one
That overflows the noon
With her cherubic quantity,
As April has begun.

The robin is the one
That speechless from her nest
Submits that home and certainty
And sanctity are best.

EMILY DICKINSON

Emily Dickinson, one of America's great poets, spent almost her entire life in Amherst, Massachussetts. Only six poems were published during her lifetime, but after she died more than a thousand were found in manuscript. Some of them are included in this book.

Alfred Tennyson, First Baron Tennyson, is considered the greatest of England's Poet Laureates. He wrote many different kinds of poems and excelled at them all. "The Owl" is an example of his short, musical lyrics.

THE OWL

When cats run home and light is come,
 And dew is cold upon the ground,
And the far-off stream is dumb,
 And the whirring sail goes round,
 And the whirring sail goes round;
  Alone and warming his five wits,
  The white owl in the belfry sits.

When merry milkmaids click the latch,
 And rarely smells the new-mown hay,
And the cock hath sung beneath the thatch
 Twice or thrice his roundelay,
 Twice or thrice his roundelay;
  Alone and warming his five wits,
  The white owl in the belfry sits.

ALFRED, LORD TENNYSON

THE VULTURE

The Vulture eats between his meals
    And that's the reason why
He very, very rarely feels
    As well as you and I.

His eye is dull, his head is bald,
    His neck is growing thinner.
Oh! what a lesson for us all
    To only eat at dinner!

            HILAIRE BELLOC

THE EAGLE

He clasps the crag with crooked hands;
Close to the sun in lonely lands,
Ringed with the azure world, he stands.

The wrinkled sea beneath him crawls;
He watches from his mountain walls,
And like a thunderbolt he falls.

ALFRED, LORD TENNYSON

Christina Georgina
Rossetti, who is among the
great English poets, was
born in London. Her father
was Italian and her mother
half Italian. She was
educated at home and spoke
Italian as fluently as
English. From childhood,
however, her health was
bad and she spent much of
her life as an invalid within
the family circle. Although
she was timid and cloistered,
in her poetry her spirit
soared to greatness.

CATERPILLAR

Brown and furry
Caterpillar in a hurry,
Take your walk
To the shady leaf, or stalk,
Or what not,
Which may be the chosen spot.
No toad spy you,
Hovering bird of prey pass by you;
Spin and die,
To live again a butterfly.

CHRISTINA ROSSETTI

THE BUTTERFLY'S DAY

From cocoon forth a butterfly
As lady from her door
Emerged—a summer afternoon—
Repairing everywhere,

Without design, that I could trace,
Except to stray abroad
On miscellaneous enterprise
The clovers understood.

Her pretty parasol was seen
Contracting in a field
Where men made hay, then struggling hard
With an opposing cloud,

Where parties, phantom as herself,
To Nowhere seemed to go
In purposeless circumference,
As 't were a tropic show.

And notwithstanding bee that worked,
And flower that zealous blew,
This audience of idleness
Disdained them, from the sky,

Till sundown crept, a steady tide,
And men that made the hay,
And afternoon, and butterfly,
Extinguished in its sea.

EMILY DICKINSON

William Wordsworth is one of English literature's most important and original poets. He is particularly renowned for his nature poetry.

TO A BUTTERFLY

I've watched you now a full half hour
Self-poised upon that yellow flower;
And, little butterfly, indeed,
I know not if you sleep or feed.

How motionless!—not frozen seas
    More motionless; and then,
What joy awaits you when the breeze
Hath found you out among the trees,
    And calls you forth again!

This plot of orchard ground is ours,
My trees they are, my sister's flowers;
Here rest your wings when they are weary,
Here lodge as in a sanctuary!

Come to us often, fear no wrong,
    Sit near us on the bough!
We'll talk of sunshine and of song,
And summer days when we were young;
Sweet childish days that were as long
    As twenty days are now.

WILLIAM WORDSWORTH

THE FLY

Little fly,
Thy summer's play
My thoughtless hand
Has brush'd away.

Am not I
A fly like thee?
Or art not thou
A man like me?

For I dance,
And drink, & sing;
Till some blind hand
Shall brush my wing.

If thought is life
And strength & breath,
And the want
Of thought is death;

Then am I
A happy fly,
If I live
Or if I die.

WILLIAM BLAKE

FIREFLIES

Little lamps of the dusk,
    You fly low and gold
When the summer evening
    Starts to unfold.
So that all the insects,
    Now, before you pass,
Will have light to see by,
    Undressing in the grass.

But when the night has flowered,
    Little lamps agleam,
You fly over treetops
    Following a dream.
Men wonder from their windows
    That a firefly goes so far—
They do not know your longing
    To be a shooting star.

CAROLYN HALL

THE BEE

Like trains of cars on tracks of plush
    I hear the level bee:
A jar across the flowers goes,
    Their velvet masonry.

Withstands until the sweet assault
    Their chivalry consumes,
While he, victorious, tilts away
    To vanquish other blooms.

His feet are shod with gauze,
    His helmet is of gold;
His breast, a single onyx
    With chrysoprase, inlaid.

His labor is a chant,
    His idleness a tune;
Oh, for a bee's experience
    Of clovers and of noon!

EMILY DICKINSON

John Keats, an Englishman, wrote many great poems before his death at the age of twenty-five. His poems are exceptionally clear and simple and he had the ability to draw the reader into a world of beautiful sounds and images.

ON THE GRASSHOPPER AND THE CRICKET

The poetry of earth is never dead:
When all the birds are faint with the hot sun,
And hide in cooling trees, a voice will run
From hedge to hedge about the new-mown mead;
That is the Grasshopper's—he takes the lead
In summer luxury,—he has never done
With his delights; for when tired out with fun
He rests at ease beneath some pleasant weed.
The poetry of earth is ceasing never:
On a lone winter evening, when the frost
Has wrought a silence, from the stove there shrills
The Cricket's song, in warmth increasing ever,
And seems to one in drowsiness half lost,
The Grasshopper's among some grassy hills.

JOHN KEATS

THE CHAMELEON

The chameleon changes his color;
    He can look like a tree or a wall;
He is timid and shy and he hates to be seen,
So he simply sits down on the grass and grows green,
    And pretends he is nothing at all.

I wish I could change my complexion
    To purple or orange or red:
I wish I could look like the arm of a chair
So nobody ever would know I was there
    When they wanted to put me to bed.

I wish I could be a chameleon
    And look like a lily or rose;
I'd lie on the apples and peaches and pears,
But not on Aunt Margaret's yellowy chairs—
    I should have to be careful of those.

The chameleon's life is confusing;
    He is used to adventure and pain;
But if he ever sat on Aunt Maggie's cretonne
And found what a curious color he'd gone,
    I don't think he'd do it again.

A. P. HERBERT

THE SNAKE

A narrow fellow in the grass
Occasionally rides;
You may have met him—did you not,
His notice sudden is.

The grass divides as with a comb,
A spotted shaft is seen;
And then it closes at your feet
And opens further on.

He likes a boggy acre,
A floor too cool for corn.
Yet when a child, and barefoot,
I more than once, at morn,

Have passed, I thought, a whip-lash
Unbraiding in the sun,—
When, stooping to secure it,
It wrinkled, and was gone.

Several of nature's people
I know, and they know me;
I feel for them a transport
Of cordiality;

But I never met this fellow,
Attended or alone,
Without a tighter breathing,
And zero at the bone.

EMILY DICKINSON

THE FROG

Be kind and tender to the Frog
    And do not call him names,
As "Slimy-skin," or "Polly-wog,"
    Or likewise "Uncle James,"
Or "Gape-a-grin," or "Toad-gone-wrong,"
    Or "Billy Bandy-knees":
The frog is justly sensitive
    To epithets like these.

No animal will more repay
    A treatment kind and fair,
At least, so lonely people say
Who keep a frog (and by the way,
    They are extremely rare).

HILAIRE BELLOC

Hilaire Belloc was an essayist, historian, novelist, and poet, but he is best known today for his light verse. His mother was English and his father French and he was educated in England. This poem about the frog is from his book Bad Child's Book of Beasts.

Charles Lamb was born in London in 1775 and lived there for his whole life. He held a number of government jobs, and wrote poetry and essays. He is best-known today for Tales of Shakespeare, *the children's book which he wrote with his sister, Mary.*

THE SNAIL

The frugal snail, with forecast of repose,
Carries his house with him wherever he goes,
Peeps out—and if there comes a shower of rain,
Retreats to his small domicile amain.
Touch but a tip of him, a horn—'tis well—
He curls up in his sanctuary shell.
He's his own landlord, his own tenant, stay
Long as he will, he dreads no Quarter Day.
Himself he boards, and lodges, both invites
And feasts himself; sleeps with himself o'nights.
He spares the upholsterer trouble to procure
Chattels, himself is his own furniture,
And his sole riches. Whereso'er he roam—
Knock when you will—he's sure to be at home.

CHARLES LAMB

A JELLY-FISH

Visible, invisible,
a fluctuating charm
an amber-tinctured amethyst
inhabits it, your arm
approaches and it opens
and it closes; you had meant
to catch it and it quivers;
you abandon your intent.

MARIANNE MOORE

*Marianne Moore was
born in St. Louis, Missouri.
She taught stenography at
the government school for
Native Americans in
Carlisle, Pennsylvania for
five years before she became
the editor of Dial magazine
in New York. Well known
for her modesty, she once
remarked, "I can see no
reason for calling my work
poetry except that there is
no other category in which
to put it."*

THE CODFISH

The codfish lays ten thousand eggs,
    The homely hen lays one.
The codfish never cackles
    To tell you what she's done.
And so we scorn the codfish,
    While the humble hen we prize,
Which only goes to show you
    That it pays to advertise.

AUTHOR UNKNOWN

THE CROCODILE

How doth the little crocodile
    Improve his shining tail,
And pour the waters of the Nile
    On every golden scale!

How cheerfully he seems to grin,
    How neatly spreads his claws,
And welcomes little fishes in,
    With gently smiling jaws!

LEWIS CARROLL

SEAL

See how he dives
From the rocks with a zoom!
See how he darts
Through his watery room
Past crabs and eels
And green seaweed,
Past fluffs of sandy
Minnow feed!
See how he swims
With a swerve and a twist,
A flip of the flipper,
A flick of the wrist!
Quicksilver-quick,
Softer than spray,
Down he plunges
And sweeps away;
Before you can think,
Before you can utter
Words like "Dill pickle"
Or "Apple butter,"
Back up he swims
Past Sting Ray and Shark,
Out with a zoom,
A whoop, a bark;
Before you can say
Whatever you wish,
He plops at your side
With a mouthful of fish!

WILLIAM JAY SMITH

William Jay Smith, an American, has written books of poems for adults, several books of children's verse, and a memoir of his childhood.

THE SHARK

A treacherous monster is the shark,
He never makes the least remark.

And when he sees you on the sand,
He doesn't seem to want to land.

He watches you take off your clothes,
And not the least excitement shows.

His eyes do not grow bright or roll,
He has astounding self-control.

He waits till you are quite undressed,
And seems to take no interest.

And when you once get in his range,
His whole demeanor seems to change.

He throws his body right about,
And his true character comes out.

It's no use crying or appealing,
He seems to lose all decent feeling.

After this warning you will wish
To keep clear of this treacherous fish.

His back is black, his stomach white,
He has a very dangerous bite.

LORD ALFRED DOUGLAS

Meet the Family

Many poets have written about their families, the things they do together, and the homes they live in. Some of the poems in this section are funny, others are serious, but they are all about members of the family—mothers, fathers, sisters and brothers, grandmothers and grandfathers, sons and daughters, and even a cousin or two.

THE READING MOTHER

I had a mother who read to me
Sagas of pirates who scoured the sea,
Cutlasses clenched in their yellow teeth,
"Blackbirds" stowed in the hold beneath.

I had a mother who read me lays
Of ancient and gallant and golden days;
Stories of Marmion and Ivanhoe,
Which every boy has a right to know.

I had a mother who read me tales
Of Gelert the hound of the hills of Wales,
True to his trust till his tragic death,
Faithfulness blent with his final breath.

I had a mother who read me the things
That wholesome life to the boy heart brings—
Stories that stir with an upward touch,
Oh, that each mother of boys were such!

You may have tangible wealth untold;
Caskets of jewels and coffers of gold,
Richer than I you can never be—
I had a mother who read to me.

STRICKLAND W. GILLILAN

AUNT SUE'S STORIES

Aunt Sue has a head full of stories,
Aunt Sue has a whole heart full of stories.
Summer nights on the front porch
Aunt Sue cuddles a brown-faced child to her bosom
And tells him stories.

Black slaves
Working in the hot sun,
And black slaves
Walking in the dewy night
And black slaves singing sorrow songs on the banks
    of a mighty river
Mingle themselves softly
In the flow of old Aunt Sue's voice,
Mingle themselves softly
In the dark shadows that cross and recross
Aunt Sue's stories.

And the dark-faced child, listening,
Knows that Aunt Sue never got her stories
Out of any book at all,
But that they came
Right out of her own life.
The dark-faced child is quiet
    Of a summer night
    Listening to Aunt Sue's stories.

LANGSTON HUGHES

Langston Hughes, the son of a lawyer, was born in Joplin, Missouri, in 1902. He was a prolific writer and was much encouraged by his mentor and fellow poet Vachel Lindsay. Many of his poems have been set to music.

WHEN MOTHER READS ALOUD

When Mother reads aloud, the past
    Seems real as every day;
I hear the tramp of armies vast,
I see the spears and lances cast,
    I join the thrilling fray;
Brave knights and ladies fair and proud
I meet when Mother reads aloud.

When Mother reads aloud, far lands
    Seem very near and true;
I cross the desert's gleaming sands,
Or hunt the jungle's prowling bands,
    Or sail the ocean blue.
Far heights, whose peaks the cold mists shroud,
I scale, when Mother reads aloud.

When Mother reads aloud, I long
    For noble deeds to do—
To help the right, redress the wrong;
It seems so easy to be strong,
    So simple to be true.
Oh, thick and fast the visions crowd
My eyes, when Mother reads aloud.

AUTHOR UNKNOWN

OUR HOUSE

Our house is small—
The lawn and all
Can scarcely hold the flower,
Yet every bit,
The whole of it,
Is precious, for it's ours!

From door to door,
From roof to floor,
From wall to wall we love it;
We wouldn't change
For something strange
One shabby corner of it!

The space complete
In cubic feet
From cellar floor to rafter
Just measures right,
And not too tight,
For us, and friends, and laughter!

DOROTHY BROWN THOMPSON

THE CHILDREN'S HOUR

Between the dark and the daylight,
When the night is beginning to lower,
Comes a pause in the day's occupations
That is known as the children's hour.

I hear in the chamber above me
The patter of little feet,
The sound of a door that is opened,
And voices soft and sweet.

From my study I see in the lamplight,
Descending the broad hall stair,
Grave Alice, and laughing Allegra,
And Edith with golden hair.

A whisper, and then a silence:
Yet I know by their merry eyes
They are plotting and planning together
To take me by surprise.

A sudden rush from the stairway,
A sudden raid from the hall!
By three doors left unguarded
They enter my castle wall!

They climb up into my turret
O'er the arms and back of my chair;
If I try to escape, they surround me;
They seem to be everywhere.

They almost devour me with kisses,
    Their arms about me entwine,
Till I think of the Bishop of Bingen
    In his Mouse Tower on the Rhine!

Do you think, O blue-eyed banditti,
    Because you have scaled the wall,
Such an old mustache as I am
    Is not a match for you all?

I have you fast in my fortress,
    And will not let you depart,
But put you down into the dungeon
    In the round tower of my heart.

And there I will keep you forever,
    Yes, forever and a day,
Till the wall shall crumble to ruin,
    And molder in dust away!

HENRY WADSWORTH LONGFELLOW

Henry Wadsworth Longfellow is one of the most popular poets who ever lived. Born in Portland, Maine, he taught modern languages at Harvard. He wrote this poem for his daughter Edith, whose golden hair is mentioned.

COMING FROM KANSAS

Whenever they come from Kansas
they stay for nearly a week
and they live with Grandma in Council Bluffs
because her house has room enough,
and we go over the day they arrive.
Everyone shouts when they pull in the drive.
We kiss and hug and I get to play
with my cousin Joan most every day
      and the grown-ups cry when they leave.

Whenever they say they're coming,
we make a lot of plans.
Joan and I like to put on a play
and we start to write it the very first day.
There're costumes and sets and curtains to do;
we write a part for the neighbor boy, too,
Denny, who comes in the very first scene
to introduce Joan, who's always the queen
      and I have to be the king.

And when it's hot in the afternoons
we get a big glass of Kool-Aid
and play cribbage or jacks on the vestibule floor
and Denny, the boy who lives next door,
comes over and dares us to go up the hill
where the cemetery, dark and still,
lies spooky with ghosts. We go before night,
but Denny and Joan always get in a fight
      and I have to take Joan's side.

Whenever they come in summer,
Joan tell me about her friends.
She says that Kansas is better, too,
there's always more fun and things to do.
But when we visited there last year
I saw her friends, and they all were queer,
And I told her so, and her face got tight
And then we had a terrible fight
 and we pulled each other's hair.

When we go to Grandma's in autumn,
Joan isn't there any more,
And Denny comes over. There's so much to do
like racing down North Second Avenue
or daring each other to slide down the eaves
or sloshing the puddles and jumping in leaves
and if we decide to write out a scene
Denny will always let me be queen
 and I don't have to bother with Joan!

MYRA COHN LIVINGSTON

MOTHER'S BIRTHDAY

Up the stairs very gently we creep,
At the door very softly we knock,
And we wonder if Mother's asleep
(We were dressed before seven o' clock).
If she thinks it's the letters or tea
What a splendid surprise it will be!

For it's only the children—it's us,
Who are standing outside at her door.
There is Sylvia and Peggy and Gus,
We three, and the baby makes four—
And we're bringing her flowers to say
"Many happy returns of the day!"

GITHA SOWERBY

MOTHER'S JEWELS

Aunt Eleanor wears such diamonds!
    Shiny and gay and grand,
Some on her neck and some in her hair,
    And some on her pretty hand.
One day I asked my mama
    Why she never wore them, too;
She laughed and said, as she kissed my eyes,
    "My jewels are here, bright blue.
They laugh and dance and beam and smile,
    So lovely all the day,
And never like Aunt Eleanor's go
    In a velvet box to stay.
Hers are prisoned in bands of gold,
    But mine are free as air,
Set in a bonny, dimpled face,
    And shadowed with shining hair!"

EUGENE FIELD

Eugene Field, an American, worked for a number of newspapers before he became a columnist for the Chicago Morning News. He was very fond of children and wrote many poems for and about them. There is a statue of Eugene Field in Lincoln Park in Chicago.

A Lesson for Mama

Dear Mama, if you just could be
A tiny little girl like me,
And I your mama, you would see
    How nice I'd be to you.

I'd always let you have your way;
I'd never frown at you and say,
"You are behaving ill today,
    Such conduct will not do."

I'd always give you jelly cake
For breakfast, and I'd never shake
My head and say, "You must not take
    So very large a slice."

I'd never say, "My dear, I trust
You will not make me say you must
Eat up your oatmeal"; or "The crust
    You'll find, is very nice."

I'd buy you candy every day;
I'd go downtown with you, and say,
"What would my darling like? You may
    Have anything you see."

I'd never say, "My pet, you know
'Tis bad for health and teeth, and so
I cannot let you have it. No—
    It would be wrong of me."

And every day I'd let you wear
Your nicest dress, and never care
If it should get a great big tear;
    I'd only say to you,

"My precious treasure, never mind,
For little clothes will tear, I find."
Now, Mama, wouldn't that be kind?
    That's just what I should do.

But Mama dear, you cannot grow
Into a little girl, you know,
And I can't be your mama; so
    The only thing to do,

Is just for you to try to see
How very, very nice 'twoud be
For you to do all this for me,
    Now, Mama, couldn't you?

SYDNEY DAYRE

Sydney Dayre was the pen name of a Mrs. Cochran, a nineteenth-century children's poet about whom almost nothing is known. Her popular poems were published in the children's magazines of the day.

MOTHER DOESN'T WANT A DOG

Mother doesn't want a dog.
Mother says they smell,
And never sit when you say sit,
Or even when you yell.
And when you come home late at night
And there is ice and snow,
You have to go back out because
The dumb dog has to go.

Mother doesn't want a dog.
Mother says they shed,
And always let the strangers in
And bark at friends instead,
And do disgraceful things on rugs,
And track mud on the floor,
And flop upon your bed at night
And snort their doggy snore.

Mother doesn't want a dog.
She's making a mistake.
Because, more than a dog, I think
She will not want this snake.

JUDITH VIORST

DADDY FELL INTO THE POND

Everyone grumbled. The sky was gray.
We had nothing to do and nothing to say.
We were nearing the end of a dismal day,
And there seemed to be nothing beyond,
     THEN
       Daddy fell into the pond!

And everyone's face grew merry and bright,
And Timothy danced for sheer delight,
"Give me the camera, quick, oh quick!
He's crawling out of the duckweed." Click!

Then the gardener suddenly slapped his knee,
And doubled up, shaking silently,
And the ducks all quacked as if they were daft
And it sounded as if the old drake laughed.

O, there wasn't a thing that didn't respond
     WHEN
       Daddy fell into the pond!

ALFRED NOYES

Alfred Noyes, an Englishman who was educated at Oxford, wrote essays, plays, novels, and short stories, in addition to poetry. He was a professor of English at Princeton University for nine years.

A BOY AND HIS DAD

A boy and his dad on a fishing trip—
There is a glorious fellowship!
Father and son and the open sky
And the white clouds lazily drifting by,
And the laughing stream as it runs along
With the clicking reel like a martial song,
And the father teaching the youngster gay
How to land a fish in the sportsman's way.

Which is happier, man or boy?
The soul of the father is steeped in joy,
For he's finding out, to his heart's delight,
That his son is fit for the future fight.
He is learning the glorious depths of him,
And the thoughts he thinks and his every whim,
And he shall discover, when night comes on,
How close he has grown to his little son.

A boy and his dad on a fishing trip—
On, I envy them, as I see them there
Under the sky in the open air,
For out of the old, old long ago
Come the summer days that I used to know,
When I learned life's truths from my father's lips
As I shared the joy of his fishing trips—
Builders of life's companionship!

EDGAR GUEST

Edgar Guest, who was born in Birmingham, England, was brought to the United States as a boy. When he was twenty, he began writing a daily poem for the Detroit Free Press. For more than fifty years these poems were syndicated to newspapers all over the country. His widely read poems were much admired for their happy quality.

THIS MORNING

This morning my father looks out of the window, rubs his nose
and says: Let's go and saw up logs
me and you.
So I put on my thick blue socks
and he puts on his army vest
and he keeps saying: Are you ready are you ready
It's a snorter of a day just look at the trees
and I run downstairs to get my old bent boots
that everybody says go round corners on their own they're
      so bent
and he comes in saying that his tobacco is like straw
which means that he is going to smoke his pipe today
So he says to Mum: We'll be back in an hour or two
which means not for ages
but Mum doesn't hear, because we lumberjacks are out of the
      door in a flash

MICHAEL ROSEN

Michael Rosen is one of Britain's most successful poets and he is extremely popular for his exuberant readings of his work. His aim is to encourage children to regard poetry as lively and entertaining.

CHOOSING A NAME

I have got a new born sister;
I was nigh the first that kissed her.
When the nursing-woman brought her
To Papa, his infant daughter,
How Papa's dear eyes did glisten!
She will shortly be to christen;
And Papa has made the offer,
I shall have the naming of her.

Now I wonder what would please her,
Charlotte, Julia, or Louisa?
Ann and Mary, they're too common;
Joan's too formal for a woman;
Jane's a prettier name beside;
But we had a Jane that died.
They would say, if 't was Rebecca,
That she was a little Quaker.
Edith's pretty, but that looks
Better in old English books;
Ellen's left off long ago;
Blanche is out of fashion now.
None that I have named as yet
Are so good as Margaret.
Emily is neat and fine;
What do you think of Caroline?
How I'm puzzled and perplexed
What to choose or think of next!
I am in a little fever
Lest the name that I should give her
Should disgrace her or defame her;
I shall leave Papa to name her.

MARY LAMB

SISTERS

"Come!" cried Helen, eager Helen.
"Time enough," cried careful Ann.
But oh, the lilac buds were swelling
And all the birds had started telling—
"Listen! look!" cried eager Helen,
Pointing where the spring began.
"Well, and what of that," said Ann.
"Something's happening—oh, let's go!"
"When it happens we shall know."
"Ah, but that's so slow!" cried Helen,
"Come on, come!" cried eager Helen.
        "Time enough," said Ann.
"I must go!" *"And I will wait.*
You'll be too soon." "You'll be too late!"
"Who knows?" said Ann. "Come on!" cried Helen,
        And ran and ran and ran.

ELEANOR FARJEON

BROTHER AND SISTER

I cannot choose but think upon the time
When our two lives grew like two buds that kiss
At lightest thrill from the bee's swinging chime,
Because the one so near the other is.
He was the elder and a little man
Of forty inches, bound to show no dread,
And I the girl that puppy-like now ran,
Now lagged behind my brother's larger tread.
I held him wise, and when he talked to me
Of snakes and birds, and which God loved the best,
I thought his knowledge marked the boundary
Where men grew blind, though angels knew the rest.
　　If he said "Hush!" I tried to hold my breath;
　　Wherever he said "Come!" I stepped in faith.

Those long days measured by my little feet
Had chronicles which yield me many a text;
Where irony still finds an image meet
Of full-grown judgments in this world perplext.
One day my brother left me in high charge,
To mind the rod, while he went seeking bait,
And bade me, when I saw a nearing barge,
Snatch out the line, lest he should come too late.
Proud of the task, I watched with all my might
For one whole minute, till my eyes grew wide,
Till sky and earth took on a strange new light
And seemed a dream-world floating on some tide—
　　A fair pavilioned boat for me alone
　　Bearing me onward through the vast unknown.

But sudden came the barge's pitch-black prow,
Nearer and angrier came my brother's cry,
And all my soul was quivering fear, when lo!
Upon the imperiled line, suspended high,
A silver perch! My guilt that won the prey,
Now turned to merit, had a guerdon rich
Of hugs and praises, and made merry play,
Until my triumph reached its highest pitch
When all at home were told the wondrous feat,
And how the little sister had fished well.
In secret, though my fortune tasted sweet,
I wondered why this happiness befell.
    "The little lass had luck," the gardener said:
    And so I learned, luck was with glory wed.

School parted us; we never found again
That childish world where our two spirits mingled
Like scents from varying roses that remain
One sweetness, nor can evermore be singled.
Yet the twin habit of that early time
Lingered for long about the heart and tongue:
We had been natives of one happy clime,
And its dear accent to our utterance clung,
Till the dire years whose awful name is Change
Had grasped our souls still yearning in divorce,
And pitiless shaped them in two forms that range
Two elements which sever their life's course.
    But were another childhood-world my share,
    I would be born a little sister there.

GEORGE ELIOT

These four sonnets are from "Brother and Sister," a sequence of eleven poems, in which the novelist George Eliot (the pseudonym of Mary Ann Evans) tells of her childhood relationship with her brother, Isaac Evans. She explored this relationship further in her novel The Mill on the Floss.

THE QUARREL

I quarreled with my brother,
I don't know what about,
One thing led to another
And somehow we fell out.
The start of it was slight,
The end of it was strong,
He said he was right,
I knew he was wrong!

We hated one another.
The afternoon turned black.
Then suddenly my brother
Thumped me on the back,
And said, "Oh, *come* along!
We can't go on all night—
I was in the wrong."
So he was in the right.

ELEANOR FARJEON

Brother and Sister

"Sister, sister go to bed!
Go and rest your weary head."
Thus the prudent brother said.

"Do you want a battered hide,
Or scratches to your face applied?"
Thus his sister calm replied.

"Sister, do not raise my wrath,
I'd make you into mutton broth
As easily as kill a moth!"

The sister raised her beaming eye
And looked on him indignantly
And sternly answered, "Only try!"

Off to the cook he quickly ran.
"Dear Cook, please lend a frying-pan
To me as quickly as you can."

"And wherefore should I lend it to you?"

"The reason, Cook, is plain to view.
I wish to make an Irish stew."

"What meat is in that stew to go?"

"My sister'll be the contents!"
            "Oh!"

"You'll lend the pan to me, Cook?"
            "No!"

Moral: Never stew your sister.

Lewis Carroll

Lewis Carroll is the pseudonym of Charles Dodgson, who for twenty-six years taught mathematics at Oxford University and wrote Alice in Wonderland for his young friend Alice Liddell.

"ONE, TWO, THREE"

It was an old, old, old, old lady,
    And a boy who was half-past three;
And the way that they played together
    Was beautiful to see.

She couldn't go romping and jumping,
    And the boy no more could he;
For he was a thin little fellow,
    With a thin little twisted knee.

They sat in the yellow sunlight,
    Out under the maple tree;
And the game they played I'll tell you,
    Just as it was told to me.

It was Hide-and-Go-Seek they were playing,
    Though you'd never have known it to be—
With an old, old, old, old lady,
    And a boy with a twisted knee.

The boy would bend his face down
    On his little sound right knee,
And he'd guess where she was hiding
    In guesses One, Two, Three.

"You are in the china closet!"
    He would laugh and cry with glee—
It wasn't the china closet,
    But he still had Two and Three.

"You are up in Papa's big bedroom,
    In the chest with the queer old key!"
And she said, "You are warm and warmer;
    But you are not quite right," said she.

"It can't be the little cupboard
    Where Mamma's things used to be—
So it must be in the little clothes press, Gran'ma,"
    And he found her with his Three.

Then she covered her face with her fingers,
    That were wrinkled and white and wee,
And she guessed where the boy was hiding,
    With a One and a Two and a Three.

And they never had stirred from their places
    Right under the maple tree—
This old, old, old, old lady
    And the boy with the lame little knee—
This dear, dear, dear, dear old lady,
    And the boy who was half-past three.

HENRY CUYLER BUNNER

Virginia Hamilton Adair has written poems all her life, but refused to publish her first book of poetry until she was eighty-three years old. This poem is about an incident in her childhood.

KEY RING

When my grandfather was very old
to one small room confined
he gave me his big bunch of keys to hold.

I asked, "Do they unlock every door there is?
And what would I find inside?"

He answered, "Mysteries and more mysteries.
You can't tell till you've tried."

Then as I swung the heavy ring around
the keys made a chuckling sound.

VIRGINIA HAMILTON ADAIR

ON THE PORCH

There used to be a way the sunlight caught
The cocoons of caterpillars in the pecans.
A boy's shadow would lengthen to a man's
Across the yard then, slowly. And if you thought
Some sleepy god had dreamed it all up—well,
There was my grandfather, Lincoln-tall and solemn,
Tapping his pipe out on a white-flaked column,
Carefully, carefully, as though it were his job.
(And we would watch the pipe-stars as they fell.)
As for the quiet, the same train always broke it.
Then the great silver watch rose from his pocket
For us to check the hour, the dark fob
Dangling the watch between us like a moon.
It would be evening soon then, very soon.

DONALD JUSTICE

Donald Justice was born in Miami, Florida, in 1925, and grew up there. He has taught at Syracuse and Iowa, as well as at the University of Florida. His poems are distinguished by their beauty and clarity.

THE NEW ENGLAND BOY'S SONG
ABOUT THANKSGIVING DAY

Over the river, and through the wood,
    To Grandfather's house we go;
        The horse knows the way,
        To carry the sleigh,
    Through the white and drifted snow.

Over the river, and through the wood,
    To Grandfather's house away!
        We would not stop
        For doll or top,
    For 'tis Thanksgiving day.

Over the river, and through the wood,
    With a clear blue winter sky,
        The dogs do bark,
        And children hark,
    As we go jingling by.

Over the river, and through the wood,
    To have a first-rate play—
        Hear the bells ring
        Ting a ling ding,
    Hurrah for Thanksgiving day!

Over the river, and through the wood—
    No matter for winds that blow;
        Or if we get
        The sleigh upset,
    Into a bank of snow.

Over the river, and through the wood,
    To see little John and Ann;
        We will kiss them all,
        And play snowball,
    And stay as long as we can.

Over the river, and through the wood,
    Trot fast, my dapple gray!
        Spring over the ground,
        Like a hunting hound,
    For 't is Thanksgiving day!

Over the river, and through the wood,
    And straight through the barnyard gate;
        We seem to go
        Extremely slow,
    It is so hard to wait.

Over the river, and through the wood—
    Old Jowler hears our bells;
        He shakes his paw
        With a loud bow wow,
    And thus the news he tells.

Over the river, and through the wood—
    When Grandmother sees us come,
        She will say, Oh dear,
        The children are here,
    Bring a pie for every one.

Over the river, and through the wood—
    Now Grandmother's cap I spy!
        Hurrah for the fun!
        Is the pudding done?
    Hurrah for the pumpkin pie!

LYDIA MARIA CHILD

Lydia Maria Child was born in Medford, Massachusetts, the daughter of a baker. When she was twenty-two years old she published a novel called Hobomok. *Two years later she began* The Juvenile Miscellany, *the first American magazine for children. This poem about Thanksgiving Day in New England is often sung.*

MANNERS

For a Child of 1918

My grandfather said to me
as we sat on the wagon seat,
"Be sure to remember to always
speak to everyone you meet."

We met a stranger on foot.
My grandfather's whip tapped his hat.
"Good day, sir. Good day. A fine day."
And I said it and bowed where I sat.

Then we overtook a boy we knew
with his big pet crow on his shoulder.
"Always offer everyone a ride;
don't forget that when you get older,"

my grandfather said. So Willy
climbed up with us, but the crow
gave a "Caw!" and flew off. I was worried.
How would he know where to go?

But he flew a little way at a time
from fence post to fence post, ahead;
and when Willy whistled he answered.
"A fine bird," my grandfather said,

"and he's well brought up. See, he answers
nicely when he's spoken to.
Man or beast, that's good manners.
Be sure that you both always do."

When automobiles went by,
the dust hid the people's faces,
but we shouted "Good day! Good day!
Fine day!" at the top of our voices.

When we came to Hustler Hill,
he said that the mare was tired,
so we all got down and walked,
as our good manners required.

ELIZABETH BISHOP

Elizabeth Bishop was seven years old in 1918 and this poem is about her own experience with her grandfather. Born in Worcester, Massachusetts, her father died before she was a year old, her mother had a breakdown and Elizabeth was raised by her grandparents. Her poems have won many awards.

SONG FOR A LITTLE HOUSE

I'm glad our house is a little house,
  Not too tall nor too wide;
I'm glad the hovering butterflies
  Feel free to come inside.

Our little house is a friendly house,
  It is not shy or vain;
It gossips with the talking trees,
  And makes friends with the rain.

And quick leaves cast a shimmer of green
  Against our whited walls,
And in the phlox the courteous bees
  Are paying duty calls.

CHRISTOPHER MORLEY

THIS IS JUST TO SAY

I have eaten
the plums
that were in
the icebox

and which
you were probably
saving
for breakfast

Forgive me
they were delicious
so sweet
and so cold

WILLIAM CARLOS WILLIAMS

Willam Carlos Williams was a poet, short-story writer, novelist, essayist, and playwright. He was born in Rutherford, New Jersey, and, except for a few stays in Europe and New York City, he spent all of his eighty years in this town. For fifty years he worked in his community as a physician, yet he always found time for his writing. For him a good poem had to be clear and simple, like this one.

TO A NEW BABY

Little kicking, cuddling thing,
You don't cry—you only sing!
Blinking eyes and stubby nose,
Mouth that mocks the budding rose,
Down for hair, peach-blows for hands—
Ah–h–h–h! Of all the "baby-grands"
Any one could wish to see,
You're the finest one for me!

Skin as soft as velvet is:
God (when you were only his)
Touched you on the cheek and chin—
Where he touched are dimples in.
Creases on your wrists, as though
Strings were fastened 'round them so
We could tie you tight and keep
You from leaving while we sleep.

Once I tried to look at you
From a stranger's point of view;
You were red and wrinkled; then
I just loved, and looked again;
What I saw was not the same;
In my eyes the blessed flame
Of a father's love consumed
Faults to strangers' eyes illumed.

Little squirming, cuddling thing!
Ere you shed each angel wing,
Did they tell you you were sent
With a cargo of content
To a home down here below
Where they hungered for you so?
Do you know, you flawless pearl,
How we love our baby girl?

STRICKLAND W. GILLILAN

MY LITTLE GIRL

My little girl is nested
    Within her tiny bed,
With amber ringlets crested
    Around her dainty head;
She lies so calm and stilly,
    She breathes so soft and low,
She calls to mind a lily
    Half-hidden in the snow.

A weary little mortal
    Has gone to slumberland;
The pixies at the portal
    Have caught her by the hand.
She dreams her broken dolly
    Will soon be mended there,
That looks so melancholy
    Upon the rocking chair.

I kiss your wayward tresses,
    My drowsy little queen;
I know you have caresses
    From floating forms unseen.
O, angels, let me keep her
    To kiss away my cares,
This darling little sleeper,
    Who has my love and prayers!

SAMUEL MINTURN PECK

TO A SAD DAUGHTER

All night long the hockey pictures
gaze down at you
sleeping in your tracksuit.
Belligerent goalies are your ideal.
Threats of being traded
cuts and wounds
—all this pleases you.
O my god! you say at breakfast
reading the sports page over the Alpen
as another player breaks his ankle
or assaults the coach.

When I thought of daughters
I wasn't expecting this
but I like this more.
I like all your faults
even your purple moods
when you retreat from everyone
to sit in bed under a quilt.
And when I say "like"
I mean of course "love"
but that embarrasses you.
You who feel superior to black and white movies
(coaxed for hours to see *Casablanca*)
though you were moved
by *Creature from the Black Lagoon*.

One day I'll come swimming
beside your ship or someone will
and if you hear the siren
listen to it. For if you close your ears
only nothing happens. You will never change.

I don't care if you risk
your life to angry goalies
creatures with webbed feet.
You can enter their caves and castles
their glass laboratories. Just
don't be fooled by anyone but yourself.

This is the first lecture I've given you.
You're "sweet sixteen" you said.
I'd rather be your closest friend
than your father. I'm not good at advice
you know that, but ride
the ceremonies
until they grow dark.

Sometimes you are so busy
discovering your friends
I ache with a loss
—but that is greed.
And sometimes I've gone
into *my* purple world
and lost you.

One afternoon I stepped
into your room. You were sitting
at the desk where I now write this.
Forsythia outside the window
and sun spilled over you
like a thick yellow miracle
as if another planet
was coaxing you out of the house
—all those possible worlds!—
and you, meanwhile, busy with mathematics.

I cannot look at forsythia now
without loss, or joy for you.
You step delicately
into the wild world
and your real prize will be
the frantic search.
Want everything. If you break
break going out not in.
How you live your life I don't care
but I'll sell my arms for you,
hold your secrets for ever.

If I speak of death
which you fear now, greatly,
it is without answers,
except that each
one we know is
in our blood.

Don't recall graves.
Memory is permanent.
Remember the afternoon's
yellow suburban annunciation.
Your goalie
in his frightening mask
dreams perhaps
of gentleness.

MICHAEL ONDAATJE

MOTHER TO SON

Well, son, I'll tell you,
Life for me ain't been no crystal stair.
It's had tacks in it,
And splinters,
And boards torn up,
And places with no carpet on the floor—
Bare.
But all the time
I'se been a-climbin' on,
And reachin' landin's,
And turnin' corners,
And sometimes goin' in the dark
Where there ain't been no light.
So, boy, don't you turn back.
Don't you set down on the steps
'Cause you finds it kinder hard.
Don't you fall now—
For I'se still goin', honey,
I'se still climbin',
And life for me ain't been no crystal stair.

LANGSTON HUGHES

Our Son

He's supposed to be our son, our hope and our pride,
In him all the dreams of our future abide,
But whenever some act to his credit occurs
I never am mentioned, the glory is hers,
And whenever he's bad or has strayed from the line,
Then always she speaks of the rascal as mine.

When trouble has come she will soberly say:
"Do you know what your son has been up to today?
Your son spilled the ink on the living-room floor!
Your son broke the glass in the dining-room door!
I am telling you now something has to be done,
It is high time you started correcting your son!"

But when to the neighbors she boasts of his worth,
It is: "My son's the best little boy on the earth!"
Accuse him of mischief, she'll just floor you flat
With: "My son, I'm certain, would never do that!
Of course there are times when he's willfully bad
But then it's that temper he gets from his dad!"

Edgar A. Guest

MY MOTHER'S HANDS

My mother's hands are cool and fair,
    They can do anything.
Delicate mercies hide them there,
    Like flowers in the spring.

When I was small and could not sleep,
    She used to come to me,
And with my cheek upon her hand
    How sure my rest would be.

For everything she ever touched
    Of beautiful or fine,
Their memories living in her hands
    Would warm that sleep of mine.

Her hands remember how they played
    One time in meadow streams,
And all the flickering song and shade
    Of water in my dreams.

Swift though her haunted fingers pass
    Memories of garden things;
I dipped my face in flowers and grass
    And sounds of hidden wings.

One time she touched the cloud that kissed
    Brown pastures bleak and far;
I leaned my cheek into a mist
    And thought I was a star.

All this was very long ago
    And I am grown; but yet
The hand that lured my slumber so
    I never can forget.

For still when drowsiness comes on
    It seems so soft and cool,
Shaped happily beneath my cheek,
    Hollow and beautiful.

ANNA HEMPSTEAD BRANCH

FOLLOWER

My father worked with a horse-plough
His shoulders globed like a full sail strung
Between the shafts and the furrow.
The horses strained at his clicking tongue.

An expert. He would set the wing
And fit the bright steel-pointed sock.
The sod rolled over without breaking.
At the headrig, with a single pluck

Of reins, the sweating team turned round
And back into the land. His eye
Narrowed and angled at the ground,
Mapping the furrow exactly.

I stumbled in his hob-nailed wake,
Fell sometimes on the polished sod;
Sometimes he rode me on his back
Dipping and rising to his plod.

I wanted to grow up and plough,
To close one eye, stiffen my arm.
All I ever did was follow
In his broad shadow round the farm.

I was a nuisance, tripping, falling,
Yapping always. But today
It is my father who keeps stumbling
Behind me, and will not go away.

SEAMUS HEANEY

JUST ME

Many poems are autobiographical. Poets often write about themselves. They write about their experiences and their dreams, as well as what they feel—happiness, sadness, excitement, even sadness. All the poems in this section fit into this category.

Rachel Field *was born in New York City and grew up in Massachussetts. She wrote many books for children as well as adult novels. Her most popular novel,* All This and Heaven, Too, *was made into a great film.*

MY INSIDE SELF

My Inside Self and my Outside Self
  Are different as can be.
My Outside Self wears gingham smocks,
  And very round is she,
With freckles sprinkled on her nose,
  And smoothly parted hair,
And clumsy feet that cannot dance
  In heavy shoes and square.

But, oh, my little Inside Self—
  In gown of misty rose
She dances lighter than a leaf
  On blithe and twinkling toes;
Her hair is blowing gold, and if
  You chanced her face to see,
You would not think she could belong
  To staid and sober me!

RACHEL FIELD

ME

As long as I live
I shall always be
My Self—and no other,
Just me.

Like a tree.

Like a willow or elder,
An aspen, a thorn,
Or a cypress forlorn.

Like a flower,
For its hour
A primrose, a pink,
Or a violet—
Sunned by the sun,
And with dewdrops wet.

Always just me.

WALTER DE LA MARE

Walter de la Mare, a gifted writer, was born in England in 1873. His family was poor and at the age of eighteen he went to work as a bookkeeper and it was not until he was thirty-six that he was able to move to the country and devote all his time to his writing. He published more than fifty volumes of poetry, short stories, essays, and novels. He is best known for his truly imaginative verse for children.

WAKING UP

Oh! I have just had such a lovely dream!
And then I woke,
And all the dream went out like kettle-steam,
Or chimney-smoke.

My dream was all about—how funny, though!
I've only just
Dreamed it, and now it has begun to blow
Away like dust.

In it I went—no! in my dream I had—
No, that's not it!
I can't remember, oh, it is too bad,
My dream a bit.

But I saw something beautiful, I'm sure—
Then someone spoke,
And then I didn't see it any more,
Because I woke.

ELEANOR FARJEON

I AM CHERRY ALIVE

"I am cherry alive," the little girl sang,
"Each morning I am something new:
I am apple, I am plum, I am just as excited
As the boys who made the Hallowe'en bang:
I am tree, I am cat, I am blossom too:
When I like, if I like, I can be someone new,
Someone very old, a witch in a zoo:
I can be someone else whenever I think who,
And I want to be everything sometimes too:
And the peach has a pit and I know that too,
And I put it in along with everything
To make the grown-ups laugh whenever I sing:
And I sing: *It is true; It is untrue;*
I know, I know, the true is untrue,
The peach has a pit,
The pit has a peach:
And both may be wrong
When I sing my song,
But I don't tell the grown-ups; because it is sad,
And I want them to laugh just like I do
Because they grew up
And forgot what they knew
And they are sure
I will forget it some day too.
They are wrong. They are wrong.
When I sang my song, I knew, I knew!
I am red, I am gold,
I am green, I am blue,
I will always be me,
I will always be new!"

DELMORE SCHWARTZ

Delmore Schwartz, poet and short story writer, was born in Brooklyn, New York. He taught in a number of universities, and was associated with a movement against academic poetry. He is best known for his short story In Dreams Begin Responsibilities, which he wrote when he was in his early twenties.

Edna St. Vincent
Millay was born in Maine
and was a graduate of
Vassar. When she was only
nineteen years old her poem
"Renascence" was published
and not long after that she
became the country's most
admired woman poet.

AFTERNOON ON A HILL

I will be the gladdest thing
    Under the sun!
I will touch a hundred flowers
    And not pick one.

I will look at cliffs and clouds
    With quiet eyes,
Watch the wind bow down the grass,
    And the grass rise.

And when lights begin to show
    Up from the town,
I will mark where must be mine,
    And then start down!

EDNA ST. VINCENT MILLAY

ONE

Only one of me
and nobody can get a second one
from a photocopy machine.

Nobody has the fingerprints I have.
Nobody can cry my tears, or laugh my laugh
or have my expectancy when I wait.

But anybody can mimic my dance with my dog.
Anybody can howl how I sing out of tune.
And mirrors can show me multiplied
many times, say, dressed up in red
or dressed up in gray.

Nobody can get into my clothes for me
or feel my fall for me, or do my running.
Nobody hears my music for me, either.

I am just this one.
Nobody else makes the words
I shape with sound, when I talk.

But anybody can act how I stutter in a rage.
Anybody can copy echoes I make.
And mirrors can show me multiplied
many times, say, dressed up in green
or dressed up in blue.

JAMES BERRY

James Berry was born in Jamaica and, although he moved to England when he was a child, he has never lost the love of storytelling and the music of language he learned there. He has written many books for children which have won major awards in England, where he now lives.

LIFE DOESN'T FRIGHTEN ME

Shadows on the wall
Noises down the hall
Life doesn't frighten me at all
Bad dogs barking loud
Big ghosts in a cloud
Life doesn't frighten me at all.

Mean old Mother Goose
Lions on the loose
They don't frighten me at all
Dragons breathing flame
On my counterpane
That doesn't frighten me at all.

I go boo
Make them shoo
I make fun
Way they run
I won't cry
So they fly
I just smile
They go wild
Life doesn't frighten me at all.

Tough guys in a fight
All alone at night
Life doesn't frighten me at all.
Panthers in the park
Strangers in the dark
No, they don't frighten me at all.

That new classroom where
Boys all pull my hair
(Kissy little girls
With their hair in curls)
They don't frighten me at all.

Don't show me frogs and snakes
And listen for my scream,
If I'm afraid at all
It's only in my dreams.

I've got a magic charm
That I keep up my sleeve,
I can walk the ocean floor
And never have to breathe.

Life doesn't frighten me at all
Not at all
Not at all.
Life doesn't frighten me at all.

MAYA ANGELOU

Maya Angelou, who wrote and recited a poem for President Bill Clinton's inauguration, has written five collections of poetry, has worked in the theater as a director, actor, and writer, was active in the Civil Rights movement, and has received many honorary degrees.

THE BOY ACTOR

Noel Coward was
an actor, composer, and a
successful writer of plays,
novels, and poems. Born in
England, from the time he
was very young his mother
encouraged his theatrical
aspirations. He began his
professional career in 1911,
when he was ten years old,
playing the part of Prince
Mussel in a play called The
Goldfish. He had very little
formal education and was
actually expelled from one
school for biting the head-
mistress's arm.

I can remember, I can remember,
The months of November and December
    Were filled for me with peculiar joys
So different from those of other boys
    For other boys would be counting the days
Until end of term and holiday times
    But I was acting in Christmas plays
While they were taken to pantomimes.
    I didn't envy their Eton suits,
Their children's dances and Christmas trees.
    My life had wonderful substitutes
For such conventional treats as these.
    I didn't envy their country larks,
Their organized games in paneled halls:
    While they made snowmen in stately parks
I was counting the curtain calls.

    I remember the auditions, the nerve-racking auditions:
    Darkened auditoriums and empty, dusty stage,
    Little girls in ballet dresses practicing "positions,"
    Gentlemen in pince-nez asking you your age.
    Hopefulness and nervousness struggling within you,
    Dreading that familiar phrase, "Thank you, dear, no more."
    Straining every muscle, every tendon, every sinew
    To do your dance much better than you'd ever done before.
    Think of your performance. Never mind the others,
    Never mind the pianist, talent must prevail.
    Never mind the baleful eyes of other children's mothers
    Glaring from the corners and willing you to fail.

I can remember, I can remember,
The months of November and December
    Were more significant to me
Than other months could ever be
    For they were the months of high romance

When destiny waited on tip-toe,
    When every boy actor stood a chance
Of getting into a Christmas show.
    Not for me the dubious heaven
Of being some prefect's protégé!
    Not for me the Second Eleven.
For me, two performances a day.

Ah those first rehearsals! Only very few lines:
Rushing home to mother, learning them by heart,
"Enter Left, through window"—Dots to mark the cue lines:
"Exit with the others"—still it was a part.
Opening performance; legs a bit unsteady,
Dedicated tension, shivers down my spine,
Powder, grease, and eye-black, sticks of make-up ready
Leichner number three and number five and number nine.
World of strange enchantment, magic for a small boy
Dreaming of the future, reaching for the crown,
Rigid in the dressing-room, listening for the call boy
"Overture Beginners—Everybody Down!"

I can remember, I can remember,
The months of November and December,
    Although climatically cold and damp,
Meant more to me than Aladdin's lamp,
    I see myself, having got a job,
Walking on wings along the Strand,
    Uncertain whether to laugh or sob
And clutching tightly my mother's hand.
    I never cared who scored the goal
Or which side won the silver cup,
    I never learnt to bat or bowl
But I heard the curtain going up.

Sir Noel Coward

THE UGLY CHILD

I heard them say I'm ugly.
I hoped it wasn't true.
I looked into the mirror
To get a better view,
And certainly my face seemed
Uninteresting and sad.
I wish that either it was good
Or else just very bad.

My eyes are green, my hair is straight,
My ears stick out, my nose
Has freckles on it all the year,
I'm skinny as a hose.
If only I could look as I
Imagine I might be.
Oh, all the crowds would turn and bow.
They don't—because I'm me.

ELIZABETH JENNINGS

JUST ME

Nobody sees what I can see,
For back of my eyes there is only me.
And nobody knows how my thoughts begin,
For there's only myself inside my skin.
Isn't it strange how everyone owns
Just enough skin to cover his bones?
My father's would be too big to fit—
I'd be all wrinkled inside of it.
And my baby brother's is much too small—
It just wouldn't cover me up at all.
But I feel just right in the skin I wear,
And there's nobody like me anywhere.

MARGARET HILLERT

SEVEN TIMES ONE

There's no dew left on the daisies and clover,
    There's no rain left in heaven:
I've said my "seven times" over and over,
    Seven times one are seven.

I am old, so old, I can write a letter;
    My birthday lessons are done;
The lambs play always, they know no better;
    They are only one times one.

O moon! in the night I have seen you sailing
    And shining so round and low;
You were bright! ah, bright! but your light is failing—
    You are nothing now but a bow.

You moon, have you done something wrong in heaven
    That God has hidden your face?
I hope if you have you will soon be forgiven,
    And shine again in your place.

O velvet bee, you're a dusty fellow,
    You've powdered your legs with gold!
O brave marsh maybuds, rich and yellow,
    Give me your money to hold!

O columbine, open your folded wrapper,
    Where two twin turtledoves dwell!
O cuckoopint, toll me the purple clapper
    That hangs in your clear, green bell!

And show me your nest with the young ones in it,
    I will not steal them away;
I am old! you may trust me, linnet, linnet—
    I am seven times one today.

JEAN INGELOW

My Shadow

I have a little shadow that goes in and out with me,
And what can be the use of him is more than I can see.
He is very, very like me from the heels up to the head,
And I see him jump before me, when I jump into my bed.

The funniest thing about him is the way he likes to grow—
Not at all like proper children, which is always very slow;
For he sometimes shoots up taller, like an India-rubber ball,
And he sometimes gets so little that there's none of him at all.

Robert Louis Stevenson

THE LAND OF COUNTERPANE

When I was sick and lay a-bed
I had two pillows at my head,
And all my toys beside me lay
To keep me happy all the day.

And sometimes for an hour or so
I watched my leaden soldiers go,
With different uniforms and drills,
Among the bedclothes, through the hills;

And sometimes sent my ships in fleets
All up and down among the sheets;
Or brought my trees and houses out,
And planted cities all about.

I was the giant great and still
That sits upon the pillow-hill,
And sees before him, dale and plain,
The pleasant land of counterpane.

ROBERT LOUIS STEVENSON

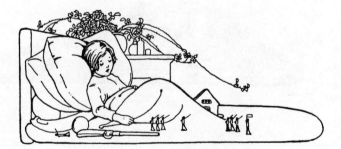

THE CENTAUR

The summer that I was ten—
Can it be there was only one
summer that I was ten? It must

have been a long one then—
each day I'd go out to choose
a fresh horse from my stable

which was a willow grove
down by the old canal.
I'd go on my two bare feet.

But when, with my brother's jack-knife,
I had cut me a long limber horse
with a good thick knob for a head,

and peeled him slick and clean
except a few leaves for the tail,
and cinched my brother's belt

around his head for a rein,
I'd straddle and canter him fast
up the grass bank to the path.

trot along in the lovely dust
that talcumed over his hoofs,
hiding my toes, and turning

his feet to swift half-moons.
The willow knob with the strap
jouncing between my thighs

was the pommel and yet the poll
of my nickering pony's head.
My head and my neck were mine,

yet they were shaped like a horse.
My hair flopped to the side
like the mane of a horse in the wind.

My forelocks swung in my eyes,
my neck arched and I snorted.
I shied and skittered and reared,

stopped and raised my knees,
pawed at the ground and quivered.
My teeth bared as we wheeled

and swished through the dust again.
I was the horse and the rider,
and the leather I slapped to his rump

spanked my own behind.
Doubled, my two hoofs beat
a gallop along the bank,

the wind twanged in my mane,
my mouth squared to the bit.
and yet I sat on my steed

quiet, negligent riding,
my toes standing the stirrups,
my thighs hugging his ribs.

At a walk we drew up to the porch.
I tether him to a paling,
Dismounting, I smoothed my skirt

and entered the dusky hall.
My feet on the clean linoleum
left ghostly toes in the hall.

Where have you been? said my mother.
Been riding. I said from the sink,
and filled me a glass of water.

What's that in your pocket? she said.
Just my knife. It weighted my pocket
and stretched my dress awry.

Go tie back your hair, said my mother,
and Why is your mouth all green?
Rob Roy, he pulled some clover
as we crossed the field, I told her.

MAY SWENSON

BLOCK CITY

What are you able to build with your blocks?
Castles and palaces, temples and docks.
Rain may keep raining, and others go roam,
But I can be happy and building at home,

Let the sofa be mountains, the carpet be sea,
There I'll establish a city for me:
A church and a mill and a palace beside,
And a harbor as well where my vessels may ride.

Great is the palace with pillar and wall,
A sort of a tower on the top of it all,
And steps coming down in an orderly way
To where my toy vessels lie safe in the bay.

This one is sailing and that one is moored:
Hark to the song of the sailors on board!
And see, on the steps of my palace, the kings
Coming and going with presents and things!

Now I have done with it, down let it go!
All in a moment the town is laid low.
Block upon block lying scattered and free,
What is there left of my town by the sea?

Yet as I saw it, I see it again,
The church and the palace, the ships and the men,
And as long as I live and where'er I may be,
I'll always remember my town by the sea.

ROBERT LOUIS STEVENSON

THE INVISIBLE PLAYMATE

When the other children go,
    Though there's no one seems to see
And there's no one seems to know,
    Fanny comes and plays with me.

She has yellow curly hair
    And her dress is always blue.
And she always plays quite fair
    Everything I tell her to.

People say she isn't there—
    They step over her at play
And they sit down in her chair
    In the very rudest way.

It is queer they cannot know
    When she's there for me to see!
When the other children go
    Fanny comes and plays with me.

MARGARET WIDDEMER

CRYING

Crying only a little bit
is no use. You must cry
until your pillow is soaked!
Then you can get up and laugh.
Then you can jump in the shower
and splash–splash–splash!
Then you can throw open your window
and, "Ha ha! ha ha!"
And if people say, "Hey,
what's going on up there?"
"Ha ha!" sing back, "Happiness
was hiding in the last tear!
I wept it! Ha ha!"

GALWAY KINNELL

SINCE HANNA
MOVED AWAY

The tires on my bike are flat.
The sky is grouchy gray,
At least it sure feels like that
Since Hanna moved away.

Chocolate ice cream tastes like prunes.
December's come to stay.
They've taken back the Mays and Junes
 Since Hanna moved away.

Flowers smell like halibut.
Velvet feels like hay.
Every handsome dog's a mutt
Since Hanna moved away.

Nothing's fun to laugh about.
Nothing's fun to play.
They call me, but I won't come out
Since Hanna moved away.

JUDITH VIORST

HOMEWORK

What is it about homework
That makes me want to write
My Great Aunt Myrt to thank her for
The sweater that's too tight?

What is it about homework
That makes me pick up socks
That stink from days and days of wear,
Then clean the litter box?

What is it about homework
That makes me volunteer
To take the garbage out before
The bugs and flies appear?

What is it about homework
That makes me wash my hair
And take an hour combing out
The snags and tangles there?

What is it about homework?
You know, I wish I knew,
'Cause nights when I've got homework
I've got much too much to do!

JANE YOLEN

GOOD LUCK GOLD

When I was a baby
one month old,
my grandparents gave me
good luck gold:
a golden ring
so soft it bends,
a golden necklace
hooked at the ends,
a golden bracelet
with coins that say
I will be rich
and happy someday.

I wish that gold
would work real soon,
I need my luck
this afternoon.

JANET S. WONG

AUGUST

Deep in the wood I made a house
    Where no one knew the way;
I carpeted the floor with moss,
    And there I loved to play.

I heard the bubbling of the brook;
    At times an acorn fell,
And far away a robin sang
    Deep in a lonely dell.

I set a rock with acorn cups;
    So quietly I played
A rabbit hopped across the moss,
    And did not seem afraid.

That night before I went to bed
    I at my window stood,
And thought how dark my house must be
    Down in the lonesome wood.

KATHARINE PYLE

LEARNING TO SEE

When they discovered I needed glasses, I was already
accustomed to blur. Everything had that vague,
hazy look satin gets as it shreds.

Grass was the first thing I saw:
stiff fringe, no longer a blur of green;
dirt, glass, brick.

When the façade of a building broke down into sections
I lost a kind of wholeness.
Things began to fracture.

Edges became visible.
I missed the haze,
rainbows in puddles when the colors merged,

mothers and their children.
There was a sharpness I lacked
steady as sound.

If I squinted or lifted the corners of my eyes,
the world clicked into focus.
Glasses were different. They slid

down my nose making the world
slip. Their boundaries visible, elliptic
blue with stars at the edges.

DONNA MASINI

IN THE SUMMER WHEN I GO TO BED

Thomas Hood, who wrote this poem, was an Englishman who lived more than one hundred years ago. His father, who was also a writer, had the same name and so he was known as Thomas, the younger, or Tom. He wrote novels for adults and also wrote and illustrated many books for children.

In the summer when I go to bed
The sun still streaming overhead
My bed becomes so small and hot
With sheets and pillow in a knot,
And then I lie and try to see
The things I'd really like to be.

I think I'd be a glossy cat
A little plump, but not too fat.
I'd never touch a bird or mouse
I'm much too busy round the house.

And then a fierce and hungry hound
The king of dogs for miles around;
I'd chase the postman just for fun
To see how quickly he could run.

Perhaps I'd be a crocodile
Within the marshes of the Nile
And paddle in the riverbed
With dripping mud caps on my head.

Or maybe next a mountain goat
With shaggy whiskers at my throat,
Leaping streams and jumping rocks
In stripey pink and purple socks.

Or else I'd be a polar bear
And on an iceberg make my lair;
I'd keep a shop in Baffin Sound
To sell icebergs by the pound.

And then I'd be a wise old frog
Squatting on a sunken log,
I'd teach the fishes lots of games
And how to read and write their names.

An Indian lion then I'd be
And lounge about on my settee;
I'd feed on nothing but bananas
And spend all day in my pajamas.

I'd like to be a tall giraffe
Making lots of people laugh,
I'd do a tap dance in the street
With little bells upon my feet.

And then I'd be a fozy fox
Streaking through the hollyhocks,
Horse or hound would ne'er catch me
I'm a master of disguise, you see.

I think I'd be a chimpanzee
With musical ability,
I'd play a silver clarinet
Or form a Monkey String Quartet.

And then a snake with scales of gold
Guarding hoards of wealth untold,
No thief would dare to steal a pin—
But friends of mine I would let in.

But then before I really know
Just what I'd be or where I'd go
My bed becomes so wide and deep
And all my thoughts are fast asleep.

THOMAS HOOD

ESCAPE AT BEDTIME

The lights from the parlor and kitchen shone out
    Through the blinds and the windows and bars;
And high overhead and all moving about,
    There were thousands of millions of stars.
There ne'er were such thousands of leaves on a tree,
    Nor of people in church or the park,
As the crowds of the stars that looked down upon me,
    And that glittered and winked in the dark.

The Dog, and the Plough, and the Hunter, and all,
    And the star of the sailor, and Mars,
These shone in the sky, and the pail by the wall
    Would be half full of water and stars.
They saw me at last, and they chased me with cries,
    And they soon had me packed into bed;
But the glory kept shining and bright in my eyes,
    And the stars going round in my head.

ROBERT LOUIS STEVENSON

FRIENDSHIP AND LOVE

∾ One of the poems in this section tells of eating hot dogs with a friend, another of two boys exploring the countryside. One poem describes the difference between love and friendship. Also included are some of the greatest love poems ever written.

A BOY'S SONG

Where the pools are bright and deep,
Where the gray trout lies asleep,
Up the river and o'er the lea—
That's the way for Billy and me.

Where the blackbird sings the latest,
Where the hawthorn blooms the sweetest,
Where the nestlings chirp and flee—
That's the way for Billy and me.

Where the mowers mow the cleanest,
Where the hay lies thick and greenest,
There to trace the homeward bee—
That's the way for Billy and me.

Where the hazel bank is steepest,
Where the shadow lies the deepest,
Where the clustering nuts fall free—
That's the way for Billy and me.

Why the boys should drive away
Little maidens from their play,
Or love to banter and fight so well,
That's the thing I never could tell.

But this I know: I love to play,
Through the meadow, among the hay.
Up the water and o'er the lea,
That's the way for Billy and me.

JAMES HOGG

MILLIONS OF STRAWBERRIES

Marcia and I went over the curve,
Eating our way down
Jewels of strawberries we didn't deserve,
Eating our way down.
Till our hands were sticky, and our lips painted,
And over us the hot day fainted,
And we saw snakes,
And got scratched,
And a lust overcame us for the red unmatched
Small buds of berries,
Till we lay down—
Eating our way down—
And rolled in the berries like two little dogs,
Rolled
In the late gold.
And gnats hummed,
And it was cold,
And home we went, home without a berry,
Painted red and brown,
Eating our way down.

GENEVIEVE TAGGARD

LAUGHING SONG

When the green woods laugh with the voice of joy,
And the dimpling stream runs laughing by;
When the air does laugh with our merry wit,
And the green hill laughs with the noise of it;

When the meadows laugh with lively green,
And the grasshopper laughs in the merry scene;
When Mary and Susan and Emily
With their sweet round mouths sing "Ha, ha, he!"

When the painted birds laugh in the shade,
When our table with cherries and nuts is spread:
Come live, and be merry, and join with me,
To sing the sweet chorus of "Ha, Ha, he!"

WILLIAM BLAKE

GOOD HOT DOGS

for Kiki

Fifty cents apiece
To eat our lunch
We'd run
Straight from school
Instead of home
Two blocks
Then the store
That smelled like steam
You ordered
Because you had the money
Two hotdogs and two pops for here
Everything on the hot dogs
Except pickle lily
Dash those hot dogs
Into buns and splash on
All the good stuff
Yellow mustard and onions
And french fries piled on top all
Rolled up in a piece of wax
Paper for us to hold hot
In our hands
Quarters on the counter
Sit down
Good hot dogs
We'd eat
Fast till there was nothing left
But salt and poppy seeds even
The little burnt tips
Of french fries
We'd eat
You humming
And me swinging my legs.

SANDRA CISNEROS

Sandra Cisneros was born in Chicago in 1954. She is the author of two books of short stories and a collection of poems. She now lives in San Antonio, Texas and is writing a novel.

Robert Frost was born in San Francisco, but he moved to New England when he was ten years old and thus became the New England poet of the twentieth century.

THE PASTURE

I'm going out to clean the pasture spring;
I'll only stop to rake the leaves away
(And wait to watch the water clear, I may):
I sha'nt be gone long. —You come too.

I'm going out to fetch the little calf
That's standing by the mother. It's so young,
It totters when she licks it with her tongue.
I sha'nt be gone long.—You come too.

ROBERT FROST

WHAT JENNY KNOWS

"I didn't come out my mummy's tummy.
No I didn't," I say to my pal Jenny.
But Jenny says, "you must have.
How come?" And I replies,

"I just didn't. Get it. I didn't."
"Everybody does," says Jenny,
who is fastly becoming an enemy.
"Rubbish," I say. "My mummy got me.

She picked me. She collected me.
I was in a supermarket,
on the shelf and she took me off it."
"Nonsense," says Jenny. "Lies."

"Are you calling me a liar?"
I'm getting angry. It's not funny.
"No, but you have a tendency"
(a word from her aunty, probably)

"To make things up."
"Look. I'm speaking the Truth."
I say, "Cross my heart."
"Don't hope to die," shouts Jenny.

Awful superstitious, so she is.
"I'm adopted," I says, "adopted."
"I know That!" says Jenny,
"But you still came out

Somebody's tummy. Somebody
had to have you. Didn't they?"
"Not my mummy. Not my mummy," I says.
"Shut your face. Shut your face."

JACKIE KAY

Leigh Hunt was a London journalist, essayist, and poet who crusaded for the abolition of slavery and child labor and was jailed for two years. This rondeau is one of his most popular poems. He wrote it for Jenny Carlyle, the wife of his friend Thomas, who was so delighted to see him after he had been ill for some weeks that she jumped up and kissed him.

RONDEAU

Jenny kissed me when we met,
 Jumping from the chair she sat in;
Time, you thief, who loves to get
 Sweets into your list, put that in:
Say I'm weary, say I'm sad,
 Say that health and wealth have missed me,
Say I'm growing old, but add,
 Jenny kissed me.

LEIGH HUNT

MAGGIE AND MILLY
AND MOLLY AND MAY

maggie and millie and molly and may
went down to the beach(to play one day)

and maggie discovered a shell that sang
so sweetly she couldn't remember her troubles, and

millie befriended a stranded star
whose rays five languid fingers were;

and molly was chased by a horrible thing
which raced sideways while blowing bubbles: and

may came home with a smooth round stone
as small as a world and as large as alone.

For whatever we lose (like a you or a me)
it's always ourselves we find in the sea.

E. E. CUMMINGS

E. E. Cummings, one of the major poets of the twentieth century, was famous for writing poems that displayed technical ingenuity, playfulness, extraordinary lyricism, and departed from traditional poetic structures. He rebelled against the conventional rules of punctuation, as is evident in this poem.

LOVE AND FRIENDSHIP

Love is like the wild rose briar,
Friendship is like the holly tree—
The holly is dark when the rose briar blooms
But which will bloom more constantly?

The wild rose briar is sweet in spring,
Its summer blossoms scent the air;
Yet wait till winter comes again
And who will call the wild briar fair?

Then scorn the silly rose wreath now
And deck thee with the holly's sheen,
That when December blights thy brow
He still may leave thy garland green.

EMILY BRONTË

POEM

I loved my friend.
He went away from me.
There's nothing more to say.
The poem ends,
Soft as it began—
I loved my friend.

LANGSTON HUGHES

LOVE

I love you, I like you,
I really do like you.
I do not want to strike you,
I do not want to shove you.
I do want to like you,
I do want to love you;
And like you and love you
And love you and love you.

WILLIAM JAY SMITH

Robert Burns is Scotland's national poet. On January 25th, his birthday, Burns Night is celebrated by Scottish people all over the world. Burns was a laborer and plowman, first on his father's and later on his own unsuccessful farms. But he spent any leisure time he had writing poetry and songs. This poem is one of his most popular.

MY LOVE IS LIKE A RED RED ROSE

My love is like a red red rose
    That's newly sprung in June:
My love is like the melody
    That's sweetly play'd in tune.

As fair art thou, my bonnie lass,
    So deep in love am I:
And I will love thee still, my dear,
    Till a' the seas gang dry.

Till a' the seas gang dry, my dear,
    And the rocks melt wi' the sun:
And I will love thee still, my dear;
    While the sands o' life shall run.

And fare thee weel, my only love,
    And fare thee weel a while!
And I will come again, my love,
    Tho' it were ten thousand mile.

ROBERT BURNS

ROMANCE

I will make you brooches and toys for your delight
Of bird-song at morning and star-shine at night.
I will make a palace fit for you and me,
Of green days in forests and blue days at sea.

I will make my kitchen, and you shall keep your room,
Where white flows the river and bright blows the broom,
And you shall wash your linen and keep your body white
In rainfall at morning and dewfall at night.

And this shall be for music, when no one else is near,
The fine song for singing, the rare song to hear!
That only I remember, that only you admire,
Of the broad road that stretches and the roadside fire.

ROBERT LOUIS STEVENSON

How do I love thee?

How do I love thee? Let me count the ways.
I love thee to the depth and breadth and height
My soul can reach, when feeling out of sight
For the ends of being and ideal grace.
I love thee to the level of every day's
Most quiet need, by sun and candlelight.
I love thee freely, as men strive for right;
I love thee purely, as they turn from praise.
I love thee with the passion put to use
In my old griefs, and with my childhood's faith.
I love thee with a love I seemed to lose
With my lost saints—I love thee with the breath,
Smiles, tears, of all my life!—and, if God choose,
I shall but love thee better after death.

ELIZABETH BARRETT BROWNING

An invalid living in London under the possessive eye of her father, who refused to allow any of his children to marry, Elizabeth Barrett invited Robert Browning to visit her after they had corresponded for many months. They married secretly and eventually settled in Italy. This sonnet was the next to last of the forty-three "Sonnets from the Portuguese," which she wrote during their courtship (he called her his "little Portuguese" because of her olive skin), but kept them secret from him until they had been married for three years.

SONNET 18

Shall I compare thee to a summer's day?
Thou art more lovely and more temperate:
Rough winds do shake the darling buds of May,
And summer's lease hath all too short a date:
Sometimes too hot the eye of heaven shines,
And often is his good complexion dimm'd:
And every fair from fair sometimes declines,
By chance, or nature's changing course untrimmed;
But thy eternal summer shall not fade,
Nor lose possession of that fair thou ow'st,
Nor shall death brag thou wander'st in his shade,
When in eternal lines to time thou grow'st;
    So long as men can breathe, or eyes can see,
    So long lies this, and this gives life to thee.

WILLIAM SHAKESPEARE

William Shakespeare wrote a sequence of one hundred and fifty-four sonnets which were first published in 1609. This poem, the eighteenth, is one of the loveliest and most popular.

THE SHEPHERD TO HIS LOVE

*Christopher Marlowe
was born in Canterbury,
England, in 1564, educated
at Cambridge University,
and killed, in a quarrel over
a bill at a tavern, when he
was only twenty-nine years
old. In his short life he wrote
six outstanding plays and
many poems, including this
one which was not published
until six years after his death.*

Come, live with me, and be my love,
And we will all the pleasures prove
That valleys, groves, hills, and fields,
Woods or steepy mountains, yields.

There we will sit upon the rocks,
Seeing the shepherds feed their flocks
By shallow rivers, to whose falls
Melodious birds sing madrigals.

There will I make thee beds of roses
With a thousand fragrant posies;
A cap of flowers, and a kirtle,
Embroidered all with leaves of myrtle;

A gown made of the finest wool,
Which from our pretty lambs we pull,
Fur-lined slippers for the cold,
With buckles of the purest gold;

A belt of straw, and ivy buds,
With coral clasps and amber studs:
And if these pleasures may thee move,
Come, live with me, and be my love.

The shepherd swains shall dance and sing
For they delight each May morning,
If these delights thy mind may move,
Then live with me, and be my love.

CHRISTOPHER MARLOWE

LOVE OF COUNTRY

∽ Through the ages, people have written patriotic poems. Some of these are about the country they themselves love; others are about heroic men, women, or children who did extraordinary things because of their love of their countries.

Sir Walter Scott, *Scottish novelist, poet, and critic, had polio as a child, which left him lame for the rest of his life. This poem, which is from Scott's collection of narrative poems,* The Lay of the Last Minstrel, *is often quoted, particularly the first three lines.*

LOVE OF COUNTRY

Breathes there the man with soul so dead
Who never to himself hath said:
    "This is my own, my native land"?
Whose heart hath ne'er within him burned
As home his footsteps he hath turned,
    From wandering on a foreign strand?
If such there breathe, go mark him well;
For him no minstrel raptures swell;
High though his titles, proud his name,
Boundless his wealth as wish can claim,
Despite those titles, power and pelf,
The wretch concentred all in self,
Living, shall forfeit fair renown,
And, doubly dying, shall go down
To the vile dust from whence he sprung,
Unwept, unhonored, and unsung.

SIR WALTER SCOTT

AMERICA FOR ME

'Tis fine to see the Old World, and travel up and down
Among the famous palaces and cities of renown,
To admire the crumbly castles and the statues of the kings,
But now I think I've had enough of antiquated things.

So it's home again, and home again, America for me!
My heart is turning home again, and there I long to be,
In the land of youth and freedom beyond the ocean bars,
Where the air is full of sunlight and the flag is full of stars.

Oh, London is a man's town, there's power in the air;
And Paris is a woman's town, with flowers in her hair;
And it's sweet to dream in Venice, and it's great to study in Rome;
But when it come to living there is no place like home.

I like the German fir woods, in green battalions drilled;
I like the gardens of Versailles with flashing fountains filled;
But, oh, to take your hand, my dear, and ramble for a day
In the friendly western woodland where Nature has her way!

I know that Europe's wonderful, yet something seems to lack:
The Past is too much with her, and the people looking back.
But the glory of the Present is to make the Future free—
We love our land for what she is and what she is going to be.

Oh, it's home again, and home again, America for me!
I want a ship that's westward bound to plow the rolling sea,
To the blessed Land of Room Enough beyond the ocean bars,
Where the air is full of sunlight and the flag is full of stars.

HENRY VAN DYKE

Henry van Dyke was a prominent writer, editor, and clergyman. He presided over the Brick Presbyterian Church in New York from 1883 to 1899 and was known for his spellbinding sermons. Van Dyke taught English literature at Princeton University for sixteen years and later served as the United States minister to the Netherlands and Luxembourg.

SONG OF THE SETTLERS

Freedom is a hard-bought thing—
A gift no man can give,
For some, a way of dying,
For most, a way to live.

Freedom is a hard-bought thing—
A rifle in the hand,
The horses hitched at sunup,
A harvest in the land.

Freedom is a hard-bought thing—
A massacre, a bloody rout,
The candles lit at nightfall,
And the night shut out.

Freedom is a hard-bought thing—
An arrow in the back,
The wind in the long corn rows,
And the hay in the rack.

Freedom is a way of living,
A song, a mighty cry.
Freedom is the bread we eat;
Let it be the way we die!

JESSAMYN WEST

CONCORD HYMN

By the rude bridge that arched the flood,
    Their flag to April's breeze unfurled,
Here once the embattled farmers stood,
    And fired the shot heard round the world.

The foe long since in silence slept;
    Alike the conqueror silent sleeps;
And Time the ruined bridge has swept
    Down the dark stream which seaward creeps.

On this green bank, by this soft stream,
    We set today a votive stone;
That memory may their deed redeem,
    When, like our sires, our sons are gone.

Spirit, that made those heroes dare
    To die, and leave their children free,
Bid Time and Nature gently spare
    The shaft we raise to them and thee.

RALPH WALDO EMERSON

Ralph Waldo Emerson, who is best known for his essays, lived in Concord, Massachusetts. It was there, on April 19, 1775, that the local farmers fired on the advancing British soldiers. Sixty-one years later, a monument commemorating that event was completed and the first stanza of Emerson's hymn was inscribed on it.

John Greenleaf Whittier was a Quaker, born in Massachusetts. He had little formal education and studied poetry by reading the work of Robert Burns. His first book of poetry was published when he was twenty-four years old. His poems were very popular and during his lifetime they were memorized and recited in schools around the country. This story of a heroine of the Civil War was a particular favorite.

BARBARA FRIETCHIE

Up from the meadows rich with corn,
Clear in the cool September morn,

The clustered spires of Frederick stand
Green-walled by the hills of Maryland.

Round about them orchards sweep,
Apple and peach trees fruited deep,

Fair as the garden of the Lord
To the eyes of the famished rebel horde,

On that pleasant morn of the early fall
When Lee marched over the mountain-wall;

Over the mountains winding down,
Horse and foot, into Frederick town.

Forty flags with their silver stars,
Forty flags with their crimson bars,

Flapped in the morning wind: the sun
Of noon looked down, and saw not one.

Up rose old Barbara Frietchie then,
Bowed with her fourscore years and ten;

Bravest of all in Frederick town,
She took up the flag the men hauled down;

In her attic window the staff she set,
To show that one heart was loyal yet.

Up the street came the rebel tread,
Stonewall Jackson riding ahead.

Under his slouched hat left and right
He glanced; the old flag met his sight.

"Halt!"—the dust-brown ranks stood fast.
"Fire!"—out blazed the rifle blast.

It shivered the window, pane and sash;
It rent the banner with seam and gash.

Quick, as it fell, from the broken staff
Dame Barbara snatched the silken scarf.

She leaned far out on the window sill,
And shook it forth with a royal will.

"Shoot, if you must, this old gray head,
But spare your country's flag," she said.

A shade of sadness, a blush of shame,
Over the face of the leader came;

The nobler nature within him stirred
To life at that woman's deed and word;

"Who touches a hair of yon gray head
Dies like a dog! March on!" he said.

All day long through Frederick street
Sounded the tread of marching feet:

All day long that free flag tossed
Over the heads of the rebel host.

Ever its torn folds rose and fell
On the loyal winds that loved it well;

And through the hill-gaps sunset light
Shone over it with a warm good-night.

Barbara Frietchie's work is o'er,
And the Rebel rides on his raids no more.

Honor to her! and let a tear
Fall, for her sake, on Stonewall's bier.

Over Barbara Frietchie's grave,
Flag of Freedom and Union, wave!

Peace and order and beauty draw
Round thy symbol of light and law;

And ever the stars above look down
On thy stars below in Frederick town!

JOHN GREENLEAF WHITTIER

THE BATTLE HYMN OF THE REPUBLIC

Mine eyes have seen the glory of the coming of the Lord:
He is trampling out the vintage where the grapes of wrath are stored.
He hath loosed the fatal lightning of His terrible swift sword;
　　　His truth is marching on.

I have seen Him in the watch-fires of a hundred circling camps;
They have builded Him an altar in the evening dews and damps;
I can read His righteous sentence by the dim and flaring lamps:
　　　His day is marching on.

I have read a fiery gospel writ in burnished rows of steel:
"As ye deal with my contemners, so with you my grace shall deal;
Let the Hero, born of woman, crush the serpent with his heel,
　　　Since God is marching on."

He has sounded forth the trumpet that shall never call retreat;
He is sifting out the hearts of men before His judgment seat:
Oh, be swift, my soul, to answer Him! be jubilant, my feet!
　　　Our God is marching on.

In the beauty of the lilies Christ was born across the sea,
With a glory in his bosom that transfigures you and me:
As he died to make men holy, let us die to make men free,
　　　While God is marching on.

JULIA WARD HOWE

◥ *Julia Ward Howe was born in New York in 1819, the daughter of a wealthy banker. She was an activist all her life—a suffragette and an abolitionist. During the Civil War she visited the Union Army of the Potomac and was asked to write dignified, patriotic lyrics to the tune of "John Brown's Body" which would then be used as a marching song. "The Battle Hymn of the Republic," first published in 1862, was the result.*

O CAPTAIN! MY CAPTAIN!

When President Abraham Lincoln was shot on the evening of Good Friday, April 14th, 1865, at Ford's Theatre in Washington, D.C., Whitman was at home with his family in Brooklyn, New York. He did not learn of the shooting until the next morning, when he read about it in the newspapers. This poem is from Memories of President Lincoln, a section of Leaves of Grass, Walt Whitman's monumental work.

O Captain! my Captain! our fearful trip is done,
The ship has weathered every rack, the prize we sought is won,
The port is near, the bells I hear, the people all exulting,
While follow eyes the steady keel, the vessel grim and daring;
  But O heart! heart! heart!
   O the bleeding drops of red!
    Where on the deck my Captain lies,
     Fallen cold and dead.

O Captain! my Captain! rise up and hear the bells;
Rise up—for you the flag is flung—for you the bugle trills,
For you bouquets and ribboned wreaths—for you the shores
  a-crowding,
For you they call, the swaying mass, their eager faces turning;
  Here Captain! dear father!
   This arm beneath your head!
    It is some dream that on the deck
     You've fallen cold and dead.

My Captain does not answer, his lips are pale and still,
My father does not feel my arm, he has no pulse nor will;
The ship is anchored safe and sound, its voyage closed and done,
From fearful trip the victor ship comes in with object won:
  Exult, O shores! and ring, O bells!
   But I with mournful tread,
    Walk the deck my Captain lies,
     Fallen cold and dead.

WALT WHITMAN

ABRAHAM LINCOLN
WALKS AT MIDNIGHT

(In Springfield, Illinois)

It is portentous, and a thing of state
That here at midnight, in our little town
A mourning figure walks, and will not rest,
Near the old courthouse pacing up and down,
Or by his homestead, or in shadowed yards
He lingers where his children used to play,
Or through the market, on the well-worn stones
He stalks until the dawn stars burn away.
A bronzed, lank man! His suit of ancient black,
A famous high top-hat and plain, worn shawl
Make him the quaint great figure that men love,
The prairie lawyer, master of us all.
He cannot sleep upon his hillside now.
He is among us:—as in times before!
And we who toss and lie awake for long
Breathe deep, and start, to see him pass the door.
His head is bowed. He thinks on men and kings.
Yea, when the sick world cries, how can he sleep?
Too many peasants fight, they know not why;
Too many homesteads in black terror weep.
The sins of all the warlords burn his heart.
He sees the dreadnoughts scouring every main.
He carries on his shawl-wrapped shoulders now
The bitterness, the folly, and the pain.
He cannot rest until a spirit-dawn
Shall come;—the shining hope of Europe free:
The league of sober folk, the Workers' earth,
Bringing long peace to Cornland, Alp and Sea.
It breaks his heart that kings must murder still,
That all his hours of travail here for men
Seem yet in vain. And who will bring white peace
That he may sleep upon his hill again?

VACHEL LINDSAY

Vachel Lindsay was born in Springfield, Illinois in 1879. As a young man he traveled around the United States exchanging copies of his poetry for meals and places to sleep. This poem about Abraham Lincoln is one of his most famous.

Emma Lazarus, a poet and translator, was born in New York City. She was eighteen when her first book, Poems and Translations, *was published. Her sonnet, "The New Colossus," perhaps her best-known poem, is inscribed on the pedestal of the Statue of Liberty.*

THE NEW COLOSSUS

Not like the brazen giant of Greek fame,
With conquering limbs astride from land to land;
Here at our sea-washed, sunset gates shall stand
A mighty woman with a torch, whose flame
Is the imprisoned lightning, and her name
Mother of Exiles. From her beacon-hand
Glows world-wide welcome; her mild eyes command
The air-bridged harbor that twin cities frame.
"Keep ancient lands, your storied pomp!" cries she
With silent lips. "Give me your tired, your poor,
Your huddled masses yearning to breathe free.
The wretched refuse of your teeming shore.
Send these, the homeless, tempest-tost to me,
I lift my lamp beside the golden door!"

EMMA LAZARUS

I HEAR AMERICA SINGING

I hear America singing, the varied carols I hear,
Those of mechanics, each one singing his as it should be,
    blithe and strong.
The carpenter singing his as he measure his plank or beam,
The mason singing as he makes ready for work, or leaves
    off work,
The boatman singing what belongs to him in the boat, the
    deckhand singing on the steamboat deck,
The shoemaker singing as he sits on his bench, the hatter
    singing as he stands,

The woodcutter's song, the ploughboy's on his way in the
    morning, or at noon intermission, or at sundown,
The delicious singing of the mother, or of the young wife
    at work, or of the girl singing or washing,
Each singing what belongs to him or her and to none else,
The day that belongs to the day—at night the party of young
    fellows, robust, friendly,
Singing with open mouths their strong, melodious songs.

WALT WHITMAN

I AM AN AMERICAN

I am an American.
My father belongs to the Sons of the Revolution;
My mother, the Colonial Dames.
One of my ancestors pitched tea overboard in Boston Harbor;
Another hungered with Washington at Valley Forge.
My forefathers were America in the making:
They spoke in her council halls;
They died on her battlefields;
They commanded her ships;
They cleared her forests.
Dawns reddened and paled.
Staunch hearts of mine beat fast at each new star
In the nation's flag.
Keen eyes of mine foresaw her greater glory:
The sweep of her seas,
The plenty of her plains,
The man-hives in her billion-wired cities.
Every drop of blood in me holds a heritage of patriotism.
I am proud of my past.
I am an AMERICAN.

I am an American
My father was an atom of dust,
My mother a straw in the wind,
To His Serene Majesty.
One of my ancestors died in the mines of Siberia;
Another was crippled for life by twenty blows of the knout.
Another was killed defending his home during the massacres.

The history of my ancestors is a trail of blood
To the palace gate of the Great White Czar.
But then the dream came—
The dream of America
In the light of the Liberty torch
The atom of dust became a man
And the straw in the wind became a woman
For the first time.
"See," said my father, pointing to the flag that fluttered near,
"That flag of stars and stripes is yours;
It is the emblem of the promised land.
It means, my son, the hope of humanity.
Live for it—die for it!"
Under the open sky of my new country I swore to do so;
And every drop of blood in me will keep that vow.
I am proud of my future.
I am an AMERICAN.

ELIAS LIEBERMAN

HOME THOUGHTS, FROM ABROAD

Robert Browning
wrote this poem when he
was living with his wife,
Elizabeth Barrett Browning,
in Florence, Italy, and was,
perhaps, homesick
for England.

Oh, to be in England
Now that April's there,
And whoever wakes in England
Sees, some morning, unaware,
That the lowest boughs and the brushwood sheaf
Round the elm tree bole are in tiny leaf,
While the chaffinch sings on the orchard bough
In England—now!

And after April, when May follows,
And the white throat builds, and all the swallows!—
Hark, when my blossomed pear tree in the hedge
Leans to the field and scatters on the clover
Blossoms and dewdrops—at the bent spray's edge—
That's the wise thrush; he sings each song twice over,
Lest you should think he never could recapture
The first fine careless rapture!
And though the fields look rough with hoary dew,
All will be gay when noontide wakes anew
The buttercups, the little children's dower—
Far brighter than this gaudy melon flower!

ROBERT BROWNING

IN FLANDERS FIELDS

In Flanders fields the poppies blow
Between the crosses, row on row,
That mark our place; and in the sky
The larks, still bravely singing, fly
Scarce heard amid the guns below.

We are the Dead. Short days ago
We lived, felt dawn, saw sunset glow,
Loved and were loved, and now we lie
    In Flanders fields.

Take up our quarrel with the foe;
To you from failing hands we throw
The torch; be yours to hold it high.
If ye break faith with us who die
We shall not sleep, though poppies grow
    In Flanders fields.

JOHN MCCRAE

Lieutenant-Colonial John McCrae, a Canadian poet and physician, wrote this poem during World War I, when he served as a medical officer. He died of pneumonia in a French hospital on January 28, 1918, after serving for four years on the Western front. Flanders is a region on the coast of Europe, partly in France and partly in Belgium. Thousands of Allied soldiers are buried there.

My Heart's in the Highlands

My heart's in the Highlands, my heart is not here;
My heart's in the Highlands a-chasing the deer;
Chasing the wild deer, and following the roe,
My heart's in the Highlands wherever I go.

Farewell to the Highlands, farewell to the North,
The birthplace of valor, the country of worth;
Wherever I wander, wherever I rove,
The hills of the Highlands forever I love.

Farewell to the mountains high covered with snow;
Farewell to the straths and green valleys below;
Farewell to the forests and wild-hanging woods;
Farewell to the torrents and loud-pouring floods.
My heart's in the Highlands wherever I go!

ROBERT BURNS

THE LEAK IN THE DIKE

The good dame looked from her cottage
    At the close of the pleasant day,
And cheerily called to her little son
    Outside the door at play:
"Come Peter come! I want you to go,
    While there is yet light to see,
To the hut of the blind old man who lives
    Across the dike, for me;
And take these cakes I made for him—
    They are hot and smoking yet;
You have time enough to go and come
    Before the sun is set."

Then the good-wife turned to her labor,
    Humming a simple song,
And thought of her husband, working hard
    At the sluices all day long;
And set the turf a-blazing,
    And brought the coarse, black bread;
That he might find a fire at night,
    And see the table spread.

And Peter left the brother,
    With whom all day he had played,
And the sister who had watched their sports
    In the willow's tender shade;
And told them they'd see him back before
    They saw a star in sight—
Though he wouldn't be afraid to go
    In the very darkest night!
For he was a brave, bright fellow,
    with eye and conscience clear;
He could do whatever a boy might do,
    And he had not learned to fear.

*Written in the nine-
teenth century by Phoebe
Cary, an American poet,
this story of the young hero
who saved his country from
a flood is familiar to every
Dutch child.*

Why, he wouldn't have robbed a bird's nest,
    Nor brought a stork to harm,
Though never a law in Holland
    Had stood to stay his arm!

And now, with his face all glowing,
    And eyes as bright as the day
With the thoughts of his pleasant errand,
    He trudged along the way;
And soon his joyous prattle
    Made glad a lonesome place—
Alas! if only the blind old man
    Could have seen that happy face!
Yet he somehow caught the brightness
    Which his voice and presence lent;
And he felt the sunshine come and go
    As Peter came and went.

And now, as the day was sinking,
    And the winds began to rise,
The mother looked from her door again,
    Shading her anxious eyes,
And saw the shadows deepen,
    And birds to their homes come back,
But never a sign of Peter
    Along the level track.
But she said: "He will come at morning,
    So I need not fret or grieve—
Though it isn't like my boy at all
    To stay without my leave."

But where was the child delaying?
    On the homeward way was he,
And across the dike while the sun was up
    An hour above the sea.
He was stopping now to gather flowers;
    Now listening to the sound,
As the angry waters dashed themselves
    Against their narrow bound.
"Ah! well for us," said Peter,
    "That the gates are good and strong,
And my father tends them carefully,
    Or they would not hold you long!
You're a wicked sea," said Peter;
    "I know why you fret and chafe;
You would like to spoil our lands and homes;
    But our sluices keep you safe!"

But hark! through the noise of waters
    Comes a low, clear, trickling sound;
And the child's face pales with terror,
    And his blossoms drop to the ground.
He is up the bank in a moment,
    And, stealing through the sand,
He sees a stream not yet so large
    As his slender, childish hand.
'Tis a leak in the dike! He is but a boy,
    Unused to fearful scenes;
But, young as he is, he has learned to know
    The dreadful thing that means.

A *leak in the dike!* The stoutest heart
    Grows faint that cry to hear,
And the bravest man in all the land
    Turns white with mortal fear.
For he know the smallest leak may grow
    To a flood in a single night;
And he knows the strength of the cruel sea
    When loosed in its angry might.

And the boy! He has seen the danger,
    And, shouting a wild alarm,
He forces back the weight of the sea
    With the strength of his single arm!
He listens for the joyful sound
    Of a footstep passing nigh;
And lays his ear to the ground, to catch
    The answer to his cry.
And he hears the rough winds blowing,
    And the waters rise and fall,
But never an answer comes to him,
    Save the echo of his call.
He sees no hope, no succor,
    His feeble voice is lost;
Yet what shall he do but watch and wait,
    Though he perish at his post!

So faintly calling and crying
    Till the sun is under the sea;
Crying and moaning till the stars
    Come out for company;
He thinks of his brother and sister,
    Asleep in their safe, warm bed;

He thinks of his father and mother;
    Of himself as dying, and dead;
And of how, when the night is over,
    They must come and find him at last!
But he never thinks he can leave the place
    Where duty holds him fast.

The good dame in the cottage
    Is up and astir with the light,
For the thought of her little Peter
    Has been with her all the night.
And now she watches the pathway,
    As yester-eve she had done;
But what does she see so strange and black
    Against the rising sun?
Her neighbors are bearing between them
    Something straight to her door;
Her child is coming home, but not
    As he ever came before!

"He is dead!" she cries; "my darling!"
    And the startled father hears,
And comes and looks the way she looks,
    And fears the thing she fears:
Till a glad shout from the bearers
    Thrills the stricken man and wife—
"Give thanks, for your son has saved our land,
    And God has saved his life!"
So, there in the morning sunshine
    They knelt about the boy;
And every head was bared and bent
    In tearful, reverent joy.

'Tis many a year since then; but still,
    When the sea roars like a flood,
Their boys are taught what a boy can do
    Who is brave and true and good.
For every man in that country
    Takes his son by the hand,
And tells him of little Peter,
    Whose courage saved the land.

They have many a valiant hero,
    Remembered through the years:
But never one whose name so oft
    Is named with loving tears.
And his deed shall be sung by the cradle,
    And told to the child on the knee,
So long as the dikes of Holland
    Divide the land from the sea!

PHOEBE CARY

LAUGHING
LYRICS

∾ This section is devoted to poems
that are guaranteed to make you laugh,
and laugh, and laugh. Some of them
are nonsense verse—funny because they
don't really make any sense. Others
were written about funny people, or
unlikely situations, or impossible events.
Ogden Nash, Edward Lear, and Lewis
Carroll are among the masters of light
verse whose poems are included.

THE TALE OF CUSTARD THE DRAGON

Ogden Nash is the acknowledged American master of light verse. He wrote for The New Yorker magazine and collections of his poems were published in books. When his daughters were young he wrote some humorous poems, like this one, for and about them.

Belinda lived in a little white house,
With a little black kitten and a little gray mouse,
And a little yellow dog and a little red wagon,
And a realio, trulio, little pet dragon.

Now the name of the little black kitten is Ink,
And the little gray mouse, she called her Blink,
And the little yellow dog was sharp as Mustard,
But the dragon was a coward, and she called him Custard.

Custard the dragon had big sharp teeth,
And spikes on top of him and scales underneath,
Mouth like a fireplace, chimney for a nose,
And realio, trulio, daggers on his toes.

Belinda was as brave as a barrel full of bears,
And Ink and Blink chased lions down the stairs,
Mustard was as brave as a tiger in a rage,
But Custard cried for a nice safe cage.

Belinda tickled him, she tickled him unmerciful,
Ink, Blink, and Mustard, they rudely called him Percival,
They all sat laughing in the little red wagon
At the realio, trulio, cowardly dragon.

Belinda giggled till she shook the house,
And Blink said Week! which is giggling for a mouse,
Ink and Mustard rudely asked his age,
When Custard cried for a nice safe cage.

Suddenly, suddenly they heard a nasty sound,
And Mustard growled, and they all looked around.
Meowch! cried Ink, and Ooh! cried Belinda,
For there was a pirate, climbing in the winda.

Pistol in his left hand, pistol in his right,
And he held in his teeth a cutlass bright,
His beard was black, one leg was wood;
It was clear that the pirate meant no good.

Belinda paled, and she cried Help! Help!
But Mustard fled with a terrified yelp,
Ink trickled down to the bottom of the household,
And little mouse Blink strategically mouseholed.

But up jumped Custard, snorting like an engine,
Clashed his tail like irons in a dungeon,
With a clatter and a clank and a jangling squirm
He went at the pirate like a robin at a worm.

The pirate gaped at Belinda's dragon,
And gulped some grog from his pocket flagon,
He fired two bullets, but they didn't hit,
And Custard gobbled him, every bit.

Belinda embraced him, Mustard licked him,
No one mourned for his pirate victim.
Ink and Blink in glee did gyrate
Around the dragon that ate the pyrate.

Belinda still lives in her little white house,
With her little black kitten and her little gray mouse,
And her little yellow dog and her little red wagon,
And her realio, trulio, little pet dragon.

Belinda is a brave as a barrel full of bears,
And Ink and Blink chase lions down the stairs,
Mustard is as brave as a tiger in a rage,
But Custard keeps crying for a nice safe cage.

OGDEN NASH

THE MOCK TURTLE'S SONG

◦ *This poem is from* Alice's Adventures in Wonderland, *which Lewis Carroll was inspired to write on a boat trip he made with Alice Liddell, the young daughter of the dean of the college where he taught mathematics, and her two sisters, Lorina and Edith.*

"Will you walk a little faster?" said a whiting to a snail,
"There's a porpoise close behind us, and he's treading on
     my tail.
See how eagerly the lobsters and the turtles all advance?
They are waiting on the shingle—will you come and join
     the dance?
Will you, won't you, will you, won't you, will you join
     the dance?
Will you, won't you, will you, won't you, won't you join
     the dance?

"You can really have no notion how delightful it will be,
When they take us up and throw us, with the lobsters,
     out to sea!"
But the snail replied, "Too far, too far!" and gave a look
     askance—
Said he thanked the whiting kindly, but he would not join
     the dance.
Would not, could not, would not, could not, would not join
     the dance.
Would not, could not, would not, could not, could not join
     the dance.

"What matters it how far we go?" his scaly friend replied,
"There is another shore, you know, upon the other side.
The further off from England the nearer is to France—
Then turn not pale, beloved snail, but come and join
     the dance.
Will you, won't you, will you, won't you, will you join
     the dance?
Will you, won't you, will you, won't you, won't you join
     the dance?"

LEWIS CARROLL

JABBERWOCKY

'Twas brillig, and the slithy toves,
　　Did gyre and gimble in the wabe;
All mimsy were the borogoves,
　　And the mome raths outgrabe.

"Beware the Jabberwock, my son!
　　The jaws that bite, the claws that catch!
Beware the Jubjub bird, and shun
　　The frumious Bandersnatch!"

He took his vorpal sword in hand:
　　Long time the manxome foe he sought.—
So rested he by the Tumtum tree,
　　And stood awhile in thought.

And as in uffish thought he stood,
　　The Jabberwock, with eyes of flame,
Came whiffling through the tulgey wood,
　　And burbled as it came!

One, two! One, two! And through and through
　　The vorpal blade went snicker-snack!
He left it dead, and with its head
　　He went galumphing back.

"And hast thou slain the Jabberwock?
　　Come to my arms, my beamish boy!
O frabjous day! Callooh! Callay!"
　　He chortled in his joy.

'Twas brillig, and the slithy toves
　　Did gyre and gimble in the wabe;
All mimsy were the borogoves,
　　And the mome raths outgrabe.

LEWIS CARROLL

In the first chapter of Through the Looking-Glass, *the sequel to* Alice in Wonderland, *Alice picks up a book with reversed printing and, by holding it up to the mirror she has just passed through, she reads this poem.*

A Tragic Story

There lived a sage in days of yore,
And he a handsome pigtail wore:
But wondered much, and sorrowed more,
    Because it hung behind him.

He mused upon this curious case,
And swore he'd change the pigtail's place,
And have it hanging at his face,
    Not dangling there behind him.

Says he, "The mystery I've found—
I'll turn me round,"—
He turned him round;
    But still it hung behind him.

Then round, and round, and out and in,
All day the puzzled sage did spin;
In vain—it mattered not a pin—
    The pigtail hung behind him.

And right and left, and round about,
And up and down, and in and out,
He turned; but still the pigtail stout
    Hung steadily behind him.

And though his efforts never slack,
And though he twist, and twirl, and tack,
Alas! still faithful to his back,
    The pigtail hangs behind him.

WILLIAM MAKEPEACE THACKERAY

THE YAK

As a friend to the children commend me the Yak
    You will find it exactly the thing:
It will carry and fetch, you can ride on its back,
    Or lead it about with a string.

The Tartar who dwells on the plains of Tibet
    (A desolate region of snow)
Has for centuries made it a nursery pet,
    And surely the Tartar should know!

Then tell your daddy where the Yak can be got,
    And if he is awfully rich
He will buy you the creature—or else he will not.
    (I cannot be positive which.)

HILAIRE BELLOC

MY BROTHER BERT

Pets are the hobby of my brother Bert.
He used to go to school with a mouse in his shirt.

His hobby it grew, as some hobbies will,
And grew and GREW and GREW UNTIL—

Oh don't breathe a word, pretend you haven't heard.
A simply appalling thing has occurred—

The very thought makes me iller and iller:
Bert's brought home a gigantic gorilla!

If you think that's really not such a scare,
What if it quarrels with his grizzly bear?

You still think you could keep your head?
What if the lion from under the bed

And the four ostriches that deposit
Their football eggs in his bedroom closet

And the aardvark out of his bottom drawer
All danced out and joined the roar?

What if the pangolins were to caper
Out of their nests behind the wallpaper?

With the fifty sorts of bats
That hang on his hatstand like old hats,

And out of a shoebox the excitable platypus
Along with the ocelot or jungle-cattypus?

Ted Hughes was born in western Yorkshire in England. He studied archeology and anthropology at Cambridge and served in the Royal Air Force. He had various jobs, including two years when he taught in the United States. In 1984, he was named Britain's Poet Laureate. He has published more than one hundred volumes of poems and plays, among which many are for children.

The wombat, the dingo, the gecko, the grampus—
How they would shake the house with their rumpus!

Not to forget the bandicoot
Who would certainly peer from his battered old boot.

Why it could be a dreadful day,
And what, oh what, would the neighbors say!

TED HUGHES

THE PURPLE COW

I never saw a Purple Cow,
    I never hope to see one;
But I can tell you, anyhow,
    I'd rather see than be one.

GELETT BURGESS

Gelett Burgess was born in Massachussetts, but for most of his life he lived in San Francisco. He wrote a lot of humorous fiction and poetry. This is his most famous nonsense poem. He also invented many words, like "goop" and "blurb," which are now part of the language.

ADVENTURES OF ISABEL

Isabel met an enormous bear,
Isabel, Isabel, didn't care;
The bear was hungry, the bear was ravenous,
The bear's big mouth was cruel and cavernous.
The bear said, Isabel, glad to meet you,
How do, Isabel, now I'll eat you!
Isabel, Isabel, didn't worry,
Isabel didn't scream or scurry.
She washed her hands and she straightened her hair up,
Then Isabel quietly ate the bear up.

Once in a night as black as pitch
Isabel met a wicked old witch.
The witch's face was cross and wrinkled,
The witch's gums with teeth were sprinkled.
Ho, ho, Isabel! the old witch crowed,
I'll turn you into an ugly toad!
Isabel, Isabel, didn't worry,
Isabel didn't scream or scurry,
She showed no rage and she showed no rancor,
But she turned the witch into milk and drank her.

Isabel met a hideous giant,
Isabel continued self-reliant.
The giant was hairy, the giant was horrid,
He had one eye in the middle of his forehead.
Good morning Isabel, the giant said,
I'll grind your bones to make my bread.

Isabel, Isabel, didn't worry,
Isabel didn't scream or scurry.
She nibbled the zwieback that she always fed off,
And when it was gone, she cut the giant's head off.

Isabel met a troublesome doctor,
He punched and he poked till he really shocked her.
The doctor's talk was of coughs and chills
And the doctor's satchel bulged with pills.
The doctor said unto Isabel,
Swallow this, it will make you well.
Isabel, Isabel, didn't worry,
Isabel didn't scream or scurry,
She took those pills from the pill concocter,
And Isabel calmly cured the doctor.

OGDEN NASH

Lewis Carroll, who was an ordained minister, an accomplished mathematician and classicist, and an excellent photographer, stammered and was extremely shy. His real name was Charles Lutwidge Dodgson. To create his pseudonym, he dropped his last name, reversed the order of his first and middle names and then converted them to names deriving from Latin.

THE WALRUS AND THE CARPENTER

The sun was shining on the sea,
    Shining with all his might:
He did his very best to make
    The billows smooth and bright—
And this was odd, because it was
    The middle of the night.

The moon was shining sulkily,
    Because she thought the sun
Had got no business to be there
    After the day was done—
"It's very rude of him," she said,
    "To come and spoil the fun!"

The sea was wet as wet could be,
    The sands were dry as dry.
You could not see a cloud, because
    No cloud was in the sky:
No birds were flying overhead—
    There were no birds to fly.

The Walrus and the Carpenter
    Were walking close at hand:
They wept like anything to see
    Such quantities of sand:
"If this were only cleared away,"
    They said, "it would be grand!"

"If seven maids with seven mops
    Swept it for half a year,
Do you suppose," the Walrus said,
    "That they could get it clear?"
"I doubt it," said the Carpenter,
    And shed a bitter tear.

"O Oysters, come and walk with us!"
    The Walrus did beseech
"A pleasant walk, a pleasant talk,
    Along the briny beach:
We cannot do with more than four,
    To give a hand to each."

The eldest Oyster looked at him,
    But never a word he said:
The eldest Oyster winked his eye,
    And shook his heavy head—
Meaning to say he did not choose
    To leave the oyster bed.

But four young Oysters hurried up,
    All eager for the treat:
Their coats were brushed, their faces washed,
    Their shoes were clean and neat—
And this was odd, because, you know,
    They hadn't any feet.

Four other Oysters followed them,
    And yet another four;
And thick and fast they came at last,
    And more, and more, and more—
All hopping through the frothy waves,
    And scrambling to the shore.

The Walrus and the Carpenter
    Walked on a mile or so,
And then they rested on a rock
    Conveniently low.
And all the little Oysters stood
    And waited in a row.

"The time has come," the Walrus said,
    "To talk of many things,
Of shoes—and ships—and sealing wax—
    Of cabbages—and kings—
And why the sea is boiling hot—
    And whether pigs have wings."

"But wait a bit," the Oysters cried,
    "Before we have our chat;
For some of us are out of breath,
    And all of us are fat!"
"No hurry!" said the Carpenter.
    They thanked him much for that.

"A loaf of bread," the Walrus said,
    "Is what we chiefly need:
Pepper and vinegar besides
    Are very good indeed—
Now, if you're ready, Oysters dear,
    We can begin to feed."

"But not on us!" the Oysters cried,
    Turning a little blue.
"After such kindness, that would be
    A dismal thing to do!"
"The night is fine," the Walrus said.
    "Do you admire the view?

"It was so kind of you to come!
    And you are very nice!"
The Carpenter said nothing but
    "Cut us another slice.
I wish you were not quite so deaf—
    I've had to ask you twice!"

"It seems a shame," the Walrus said,
    "To play them such a trick.
After we've brought them out so far,
    And made them trot so quick!"
The Carpenter said nothing but
    "The butter's spread too thick!"

"I weep for you," the Walrus said:
    "I deeply sympathize,"
With sobs and tears he sorted out
    Those of the largest size,
Holding his pocket handkerchief
    Before his streaming eyes.

"O Oysters," said the Carpenter,
    "You've had a pleasant run!
Shall we be trotting home again!"
    But answer came there none—
And this was scarcely odd, because
    They'd eaten every one.

LEWIS CARROLL

SIX LIMERICKS

There was an Old Man with a beard,
Who said, "It is just as I feared!
    Two Owls and a Hen,
        Four Larks and a Wren,
Have all built their nests in my beard!"

Edward Lear was a talented painter of birds, animals, and landscapes, For a time he gave drawing lessons to Queen Victoria. He did the whimsical illustrations for his own limericks, of which he wrote many.

There was an Old Man who forgot,
That his tea was excessively hot.
    When they said, "Let it cool,"
        He answered, "You fool!
I shall pour it back into the pot."

There was an Old Man who supposed,
That the street door was partially closed;
    But some very large rats,
        Ate his coats and his hats,
While that futile old gentleman dozed.

There was a Young Lady whose eyes,
Were unique as to color and size;
When she opened them wide,
People all turned aside,
And started away in surprise.

There was a Young Lady, whose nose
Continually prospers and grows;
When it grew out of sight,
She exclaimed in a fright,
"Oh! Farewell to the end of my nose!"

There was an Old Person whose habits
Induced him to feed upon rabbits;
When he'd eaten eighteen,
He turned perfectly green,
Upon which he relinquished those habits.

EDWARD LEAR

Stephen Vincent Benet wrote many short stories of which the most famous is "The Devil and Daniel Webster." Of the many poems he wrote, the most popular is "John Brown's Body." His wife, Rosemary, was also a writer and they often worked together.

A Nonsense Song

Rosemary, Rosemary, let down your hair!
The cow's in the hammock, the crow's in the chair!
I was making you songs out of sawdust and silk,
But they came in to call and they spilt them like milk.

The cat's in the coffee, the wind's in the east,
He screams like a peacock and whines like a priest
And the saw of his voice makes my blood turn to mice—
So let down your long hair and shut off his advice!

Pluck out the thin hairpins and let the waves stream,
Brown-gold as brook-waters that dance through a dream,
Gentle-curled as young cloudlings, sweet-fragrant as bay,
Till it takes all the fierceness of living away.

Oh, when you are with me, my heart is white steel.
But the bat's in the belfry, the mold's in the meal,
And I think I hear skeletons climbing the stair!
  —Rosemary, Rosemary, let down your bright hair!

STEPHEN VINCENT BENET

A TRIP TO MORROW

I started on a journey just about a week ago
For the little town of Morrow in the State of Ohio.
I never was a traveler and really didn't know
That Morrow had been ridiculed a century or so.
I went down to the depot for my ticket and applied
For tips regarding Morrow, interviewed the station guide.
Said I, "My friend, I want to go to Morrow and return
Not later than tomorrow, for I haven't time to burn."

Said he to me, "Now let me see, if I have heard you right,
You want to go to Morrow and come back tomorrow night.
You should have gone to Morrow yesterday and back today,
For if you started yesterday to Morrow, don't you see
You should have got to Morrow and returned today at three.
The train that started yesterday, now understand me right,
Today it gets to Morrow and returns tomorrow night."

"Now if you start to Morrow, you will surely land
Tomorrow into Morrow, not today you understand,
For the train today to Morrow, if the schedule is right
Will get you into Morrow by about tomorrow night."
Said I, "I guess you know it all, but kindly let me say,
How can I go to Morrow if I leave the town today?"
Said he, "You cannot go to Morrow any more today,
For the train that goes to Morrow is a mile upon its way."

AUTHOR UNKNOWN

THE PANCAKE COLLECTOR

Come visit my pancake collection,
it's unique in the civilized world.
I have pancakes of every description,
pancakes flaky and fluffy and curled.

I have pancakes of various sizes,
pancakes regular, heavy and light,
underdone pancakes and overdone pancakes,
and pancakes done perfectly right.

I have pancakes locked up in the closets,
I have pancakes on hangers and hooks.
They're in bags and in boxes and bureaus,
and pressed in the pages of books.

There are pretty ones sewn to the cushions
and tastefully pinned to the drapes.
The ceilings are coated with pancakes,
and the carpets are covered with crepes.

I have pancakes in most of my pockets,
and concealed in the linings of suits.
There are tiny ones stuffed in my mittens
and large ones packed in my boots.

I have extras of most of my pancakes,
I maintain them in rows on these shelves,
And if you say nice things about them,
you may take a few home for yourselves.

I see that you've got to be going,
won't you let yourselves out by the door?
It is time that I pour out the batter
and bake up a few hundred more.

JACK PRELUTSKY

THE OWL AND THE PUSSY-CAT

The Owl and the Pussy-Cat went to sea
    In a beautiful pea-green boat,
They took some honey, and plenty of money,
    Wrapped up in a five-pound note.

The Owl looked up to the stars above,
    And sang to a small guitar,
"O lovely Pussy! O Pussy, my love,
    What a beautiful Pussy you are, you are!
    What a beautiful Pussy you are!"

Pussy said to the Owl, "You elegant fowl!
    How charmingly sweet you sing!
O let us be married! Too long we have tarried.
    But what shall we do for a ring?"

They sailed away for a year and a day,
    To the land where the Bong tree grows,
And there in a wood a Piggy-wig stood,
    With a ring at the end of his nose, his nose,
    With a ring at the end of his nose.

"Dear Pig, are you willing to sell for one shilling
    Your ring?" Said the Piggy, "I will."
So they took it away, and were married next day
    By the Turkey who lives on the hill.

They dined on mince and slices of quince,
    Which they ate with a runcible spoon;
And hand in hand, on the edge of the sand,
    They danced by the light of the moon, the moon,
    They danced by the light of the moon.

EDWARD LEAR

Edward Lear traveled extensively—even to Egypt and India—as a watercolor painter of landscapes and birds. Among these were marvelous paintings of parrots. This poem appeared in his book Nonsense Songs, Stories, Botany, and Botany, *which was published in 1871. In his poems he often invented words, like "runcible."*

THE POBBLE WHO HAS NO TOES

Edward Lear had poor eyesight and suffered from epilepsy and asthma. He was a lonely man, often terribly depressed, and was convinced that those who met him were repelled by his ugliness. Many people, including the poet W.H. Auden, believe that he took refuge in the wonderful nonsense of his poems.

The Pobble who has no toes
    Had once as many as we;
When they said, "Some day you may lose them all,"
    He replied "Fish Fiddle-de-dee!"
And his Aunt Jobiska made him drink
Lavender water tinged with pink
For she said, "The world in general knows
There's nothing so good for a Pobble's toes!"

The Pobble who has no toes
    Swam across the Bristol Channel;
But before he set out he wrapped his nose
    In a piece of scarlet flannel.
For his Aunt Jobiska said, "No harm
Can come to his toes if his nose is warm;
And it's perfectly known that a Pobble's toes
Are safe—provided he minds his nose."

The Pobble swam fast and well,
    And when boats or ships came near him,
He tinkledy-blinkedy-winkled a bell,
    So that all the world could hear him,

And all the sailors and admirals cried,
When they saw him nearing the further side,
"He has gone to fish for his Aunt Jobiska's
Runcible Cat with crimson whiskers!"

But before he touched the shore—
    The shore of the Bristol Channel—
A sea-green porpoise carried away
    His wrapper of scarlet flannel,
And when he came to observe his feet,
Formerly garnished with toes so neat,
His face at once became forlorn
On perceiving that all his toes were gone!

And nobody every knew,
    From that dark day to the present,
Whoso had taken the Pobble's toes,
    In a manner so far from pleasant.
Whether the shrimps or crawfish gray,
Or crafty mermaids stole them away—
Nobody knew; and nobody knows
How the Pobble was robbed of his twice five toes!

The Pobble who has no toes
    Was placed in a friendly bark,
And they rowed him back, and carried him up
    To his Aunt Jobiska's park.
And she made him a feast, at his earnest wish,
Of eggs and buttercups fried with fish;
And she said, "It's a fact the whole world knows,
That Pobbles are happier without their toes."

EDWARD LEAR

SIX SILLY RHYMES

1.

Way down South where bananas grow,
A grasshopper stepped on an elephant's toe
The elephant said, with tears in his eyes,
"Pick on somebody your own size."

2.

A horse and a flea and three blind mice
Sat on a curbstone shooting dice.
The horse he slipped and fell on the flea.
The flea said, "Whoops, there's a horse on me."

3.

I asked my mother for fifty cents
To see the elephant jump the fence.
He jumped so high that he touched the sky
And never came back till the Fourth of July.

4.

The man in the wilderness asked of me,
"How many strawberries grow in the sea?"
I answered him as I thought good,
"As many red herrings as grow in the wood."

5.

Order in the court
The judge is eating beans
His wife is in the bathtub
Shooting submarines.

6.

A peanut sat on the railroad track,
His heart was all a-flutter.
Along came a train—
Toot, toot!—peanut butter!

AUTHORS UNKNOWN

THE ELF AND THE DORMOUSE

Under a toadstool crept a wee elf,
Out of the rain, to shelter himself.

Under the toadstool sound asleep,
Sat a big dormouse all in a heap.

Trembled the wee elf, frightened, and yet
Fearing to fly away lest he get wet.

To the next shelter—maybe a mile!
Sudden the wee elf smiled a wee smile.

Tugged till the toadstool toppled in two.
Holding it over him, gaily he flew.

Soon he was safe home, dry as could be.
Soon woke the dormouse—"Good gracious me!"

"Where is my toadstool?" loud he lamented,
And that's how umbrellas first were invented.

OLIVER HERFORD

Oliver Herford was born in England but came to the United States when he was nineteen years old. He was an illustrator as well as a writer of poems and stories for adults and for children.

SARAH CYNTHIA SYLVIA STOUT
WOULD NOT TAKE THE GARBAGE OUT

Sarah Cynthia Sylvia Stout
Would not take the garbage out!
She'd scour the pots and scrape the pans,
Candy the yams and spice the hams,
And though her daddy would scream and shout,
She simply would not take the garbage out.
And so it piled up to the ceilings:
Coffee grounds, potato peelings,
Brown bananas, rotten peas,
Chunks of sour cottage cheese.
It filled the can, it covered the floor,
It cracked the window and blocked the door
With bacon rinds and chicken bones,
Drippy ends of ice cream cones,
Prune pits, peach pits, orange peel,
Gloppy glumps of cold oatmeal,
Pizza crusts and withered greens,
Soggy beans and tangerines,
Crusts of black burned buttered toast,
Gristly bits of beefy roasts . . .
The garbage rolled on down the hall,
It raised the roof, it broke the wall . . .
Greasy napkins, cookie crumbs,
Globs of gooey bubble gum,
Cellophane from green baloney,
Rubbery blubbery macaroni,
Peanut butter, caked and dry,
Curdled milk and crusts of pie,
Moldy melons, dried-up mustard,
Eggshells mixed with lemon custard,
Cold french fries and rancid meat,
Yellow lumps of Cream of Wheat.

At last the garbage reached so high
That finally it touched the sky.
And all the neighbors moved away,
And none of her friends would come to play.
And finally Sarah Cynthia Stout said,
"OK, I'll take the garbage out!"
But then, of course, it was too late . . .
The garbage reached across the state,
From New York to the Golden Gate.
And there, in the garbage she did hate,
Poor Sarah met an awful fate,
That I cannot right now relate
Because the hour is much too late.
But children, remember Sarah Stout
And always take the garbage out!

SHEL SILVERSTEIN

Shel Silverstein has lived in Chicago all his life. He is a talented poet, cartoonist, composer, and folk singer. His books include The Giving Tree *and* Where the Sidewalk Ends *from where this poem is taken.*

JUDGING BY APPEARANCES

An old Jack-o'-lantern lay on the ground;
He looked at the Moon-man, yellow and round.

The old Jack-o'-lantern gazed and he gazed,
And still as he looked he grew more amazed.

Then said Jack-o'-lantern, "How can it be
That fellow up there looks so much like me?

"I s'pose he must be a brother of mine,
And somebody cut him, too, from the vine.

"He looks very grand up there in the sky;
But I know just how 'twill be, by and by.

"He's proud of his shining, I have no doubt,
But just wait until his candle goes out!"

EMILIE POULSSON

MR. NOBODY

I know a funny little man,
    As quiet as a mouse,
Who does the mischief that is done
    In everybody's house!
There's no one ever sees his face,
    And yet we all agree
That every plate we break was cracked
    By Mr. Nobody.

'Tis he who always tears our books,
    Who leaves the door ajar,
He pulls the buttons from our shirts,
    And scatters pins afar;
That squeaking door will always squeak,
    For, prithee, don't you see,
We leave the oiling to be done
    By Mr. Nobody.

The finger marks upon the door
    By none of us are made;
We never leave the blinds unclosed,
    To let the curtains fade.
The ink we never spill; the books
    That lying round you see
Are not our books—they all belong
    To Mr. Nobody.

AUTHOR UNKNOWN

THE TWINS

In form and feature, face and limb,
    I grew so like my brother,
That folks got taking me for him,
    And each for one another.

It puzzled all our kith and kin,
    It reached an awful pitch;
For one of us was born a twin,
    Yet not a soul knew which.

One day (to make the matter worse),
    Before our names were fixed,
As we were being washed by nurse
    We got completely mixed;

And thus, you see, by Fate's decree,
    (Or rather nurse's whim),
My brother John got christened me,
    And I got christened him.

This fatal likeness even dogg'd
    My footsteps when at school,
And I was always getting flogg'd,
    For John turned out a fool.

I put this question hopelessly
    To everyone I knew—
What would you do, if you were me,
    To prove that you were you?

Our close resemblance turned the tide
    Of my domestic life;
For somehow my intended bride
    Became my brother's wife.

In short, year after year the same
    Absurd mistake went on;
And when I died—the neighbors came
    And buried brother John!

HENRY S. LEIGH

THE SEVENTH SILLY RHYME

I went to the animal fair,
The birds and beasts were there.
The big baboon, by the light of the moon,
Was combing his auburn hair.
The monkey, he got drunk,
And sat on the elephant's trunk.
The elephant sneezed and fell on his knees,
And what became of the monk, the monk?

AUTHOR UNKNOWN

THREE BLIND MICE

The Whole Story

> Three small mice,
> Three small mice,
>   Pined for some fun,
>   Pined for some fun.
> They made up their minds to set out to roam;
> Said they, " 'Tis dull to remain at home,"
> And all the luggage they took was a comb,
>   These three small mice.
>
> Three bold mice,
> Three bold mice,
>   Came to an inn,
>   Came to an inn.
> "Good evening, Host, can you give us a bed?"
> But the host he grinned and he shook his head,
> So they all slept out in a field instead,
>   These three bold mice.

> Three cold mice,
> Three cold mice,
>   Woke up next morn,
>   Woke up next morn,
> They each had a cold and a swollen face,
> Through sleeping all night in an open space,
> So they rose quite early and left the place,
>   These three cold mice.

Everyone, or nearly everyone, knows the little ditty about the three blind mice. But not many people know how they lost their sight, why the farmer's wife cut off their tails, and what happened to them after that.
This poem tells the whole story of the three little mice.
It can be sung or recited.

Three hungry mice,
Three hungry mice,
  Searched for some food,
  Searched for some food,
But all they found was a walnut shell
That lay by the side of a dried-up well.
Who had eaten the nut they could not tell,
  These three hungry mice.

Three starved mice,
Three starved mice,
  Came to a farm,
  Came to a farm,
The farmer was eating some bread and cheese;
So they all went down on their hands and knees,
And squeaked, "Pray, give us a morsel, please,"
  These three starved mice.

Three glad mice,
Three glad mice,
  Ate all they could,
  Ate all they could.
They felt so happy they danced with glee;
But the farmer's wife came in to see
What might this merrymaking be
  Of three glad mice.

Three poor mice,
Three poor mice,
  Soon changed their tone,
  Soon changed their tone.
The farmer's wife said, "What are you at,
And why were you capering round like that?
Just wait a minute: I'll fetch the cat."
  Oh, dear! poor mice.

Three scared mice,
Three scared mice,
    Ran for their lives,
    Ran for their lives,
They jumped out onto the window ledge;
The mention of "cat" set their teeth on edge,
So they hid themselves in the bramble hedge,
    These three scared mice.

Three sad mice,
Three sad mice,
    What could they do?
    What could they do?
The bramble hedge was most unkind:
It scratched their eyes and made them blind,
And soon each mouse went out of his mind,
    These three sad mice.

Three blind mice,
Three blind mice,
    See how they run!
    See how they run!
They all ran after the farmer's wife,
Who cut off their tails with the carving knife.
Did you ever see such a sight in your life
    As three blind mice?

Three sick mice,
Three sick mice,
    Gave way to tears,
    Gave way to tears.
They could not see and they had no end;
They sought a doctor and found a friend.
He gave them some "Never too late to mend,"
    These three sick mice.

Three wise mice,
Three wise mice,
    Rubbed rubbed away,
    Rubbed rubbed away,
And soon their tails began to grow,
And their eyes recovered their sight, you know;
They looked in the glass and it told them so,
    These three wise mice.

Three proud mice,
Three proud mice,
    Soon settled down,
    Soon settled down.
The name of their house I cannot tell,
But they've learned a trade and are doing well.
If you call upon them, ring the bell
    Three times twice.

JOHN W. IVIMEY

THE TABLE AND THE CHAIR

Said the Table to the Chair,
"You can hardly be aware,
How I suffer from the heat
And from chilblains on my feet!
If we took a little walk,
We might have a little talk!
Pray let us take the air!"
Said the Table to the Chair.

Said the Chair unto the Table,
"Now you know we are not able!
How foolishly you talk,
When you know we cannot walk!"
Said the Table, with a sigh,
"It can do no harm to try,
I've as many legs as you,
Why can't we walk on two?"

So they both went slowly down,
And walked about the town
With a cheerful bumpy sound,
As they toddled round and round,
And everybody cried,
As they hastened to their side,
"See! the Table and the Chair
Have come out to take the air!"

But in going down an alley,
To a castle in a valley,
They completely lost their way,
And wandered all the day,
Till, to see them safely back,
They paid a Ducky-quack,

And a Beetle, and a Mouse,
Who took them to their house.

Then they whispered to each other,
"O delightful little brother!
Let us dine on Beans and Bacon!"
So the Ducky and the leetle
Browny-Mousy and the Beetle
Dined, and danced upon their heads
Till they toddled to their beds.

EDWARD LEAR

ANOTHER SILLY RHYME

Moses supposes his toeses are roses,
But Moses supposes erroneously;
For nobody's toeses are posies of roses
As Moses supposes his toeses to be.

AUTHOR UNKNOWN

Carolyn Wells, who was born in New Jersey, wrote nonsense poems, like this one, and detective novels. She also edited many collections of humorous verse.

HOW TO TELL
THE WILD ANIMALS

If ever you should go by chance
    To jungles in the East;
And if there should to you advance
    A large and tawny beast,
If he roars at you as you're dyin'
You'll know it is the Asian lion.

Or, if some time when roaming round,
    A noble wild beast greets you,
With black stripes on a yellow ground,
    Just notice if he eats you.
This simple rule may help you learn
The Bengal Tiger to discern.

If strolling forth, a beast you view,
    Whose hide with spots is peppered,
As soon as he has lept on you,
    You'll know it is the leopard.
'Twill do no good to roar with pain,
He'll only lep and lep again.

If when you're walking round your yard,
    You meet a creature there,
Who hugs you very, very hard,
    Be sure it is the bear.
If you have any doubt, I guess
He'll give you just one more caress.

Though to distinguish beasts of prey
    A novice might nonplus,
The crocodiles you always may
    Tell from hyenas thus:
Hyenas come with merry smiles;
But if they weep, they're crocodiles.

The true chameleon is small,
    A lizard sort of thing;
He hasn't any ears at all,
    And not a single wing.
If there is nothing on the tree,
'Tis the chameleon you see.

Carolyn Wells

WORDS

Now, speech is very curious:
You never know what minute
A word will show a brand-new side,
With brand-new meaning in it.
This world could hardly turn around,
If some things acted like they sound.

Suppose the April flower beds,
Down in the garden spaces,
Were made with green frog-blanket spreads
And caterpillar cases;
Or oak trees locked their trunks to hide
The countless rings they keep inside!

Suppose from every pitcher plant
The milkweed came a-pouring;
That tiger lilies could be heard
With dandelions roaring,
Till all the cattails, far and near,
Began to bristle up in fear!

What if the old cow blew her horn
Some peaceful evening hour,
And suddenly a blast replied
From every trumpet flower,
While people's ears beat noisy drums
To "Hail the Conquering Hero Comes!"

If barnyard fowls had honeycombs,
What should we think, I wonder?
If lightning bugs should swiftly strike,
Then peal with awful thunder?
And would it turn out pink cheeks pale
To see a comet switch its tail?

NANCY BYRD TURNER

CONTRARY MARY

You ask why Mary was called contrary?
Well, this is why, my dear:
She planted the most outlandish things
In her garden every year;
She was always sowing the queerest seed,
And when advised to stop,
Her answer was merely, "No, indeed—
Just wait till you see my crop!"

And here are some of the crops, my child
(Although not nearly all):
Bananarcissus and cucumberries,
And violettuce small;
Potatomatoes, melonions rare,
And rhubarberries round,
With procupineapples prickly rough
On a little bush close to the ground.

She gathered the stuff in mid-July
And sent it away to sell—
And now you'll see how she earned her name,
And how she earned it well.
Were the crops hauled off in a farmer's cart?
No, not by any means,
But in little June buggies and automobeetles
And dragonflying machines!

NANCY BYRD TURNER

~ *Hilaire Belloc was born in France of an English mother and a French father. He wrote wonderfully gruesome poems for children, like this one, which were collected in the book* Cautionary Tales.

JIM

There was a boy whose name was Jim;
His friends were very good to him.
They gave him tea, and cakes, and jam,
And slices of delicious ham,
And chocolate with pink inside
And little tricycles to ride,
And read him stories through and through,
And even took him to the zoo—
But there it was the dreadful Fate
Befell him which I now relate.

You know—at least you ought to know,
For I have often told you so—
That children never are allowed
To leave their nurses in a crowd;
Now this was Jim's especial foible,
He ran away when he was able,
And on this inauspicious day
He slipped his hand and ran away!

He hadn't gone a yard when—Bang!
With open jaws, a lion sprang,
And hungrily began to eat
The boy: beginning at his feet.
Now, just imagine how it feels
When first your toes and then your heels,
And then by gradual degrees,
Your shins and ankles, calves and knees,
Are slowly eaten, bit by bit.
No wonder Jim detested it!
No wonder that he shouted "Hi!"

The honest keeper heard his cry,
Though very fat he almost ran
To help the little gentleman.
"Ponto!" he ordered as he came
(For Ponto was the lion's name),
"Ponto!" he cried, with angry frown,
"Let go, sir! Down, sir! Put it down!"
The lion made a sudden stop,
He let the dainty morsel drop,
And slunk reluctant to his cage,
Snarling with disappointed rage.
But when he bent him over Jim,
The honest keeper's eyes were dim.
The lion having reached his head,
The miserable boy was dead!

When nurse informed his parents, they
Were more concerned than I can say:—
His mother, as she dried her eyes,
Said, "Well—it gives me no surprise,
He would not do as he was told!"
His father, who was self-controlled,
Bade all the children round attend
To James's miserable end,
And always keep a-hold of Nurse
For fear of finding something worse.

HILAIRE BELLOC

THE MAD GARDENER'S SONG

He thought he saw an elephant,
    That practiced on a fife:
He looked again, and found it was
    A letter from his wife.
"At length I realize," he said,
    "The bitterness of Life!"

He thought he saw a buffalo
    Upon the chimney-piece:
He looked again, and found it was
    His sister's husband's niece.
Unless you leave this house," he said,
    "I'll send for the police!"

He thought he saw a rattlesnake
    That questioned him in Greek:
He looked again, and found it was
    The middle of next week.
"The one thing I regret," he said,
    "Is that it cannot speak!"

He thought he saw a banker's clerk
    Descending from the bus:
He looked again, and found it was
    A hippopotamus.
"If this should stay to dine," he said.
    "There won't be much for us!"

He thought he saw a kangaroo
    That worked a coffee mill:
He looked again, and found it was
    A vegetable pill.
"Were I to swallow this," he said,
    "I should be very ill!"

He though he saw a coach and four
    That stood beside his bed:
He looked again, and found it was
    A bear without a head.
"Poor thing," he said, "poor silly thing!
    It's waiting to be fed!"

He thought he saw an albatross
    That fluttered round the lamp:
He looked again, and found it was
    A penny postage stamp.
"You'd best be getting home," he said,
    "The nights are very damp!"

He thought he saw a garden door
    That opened with a key:
He looked again, and found it was
    A double rule of three:
"And all its mystery," he said,
    "Is clear as day to me!"

He thought he saw an argument
    That proved he was the pope:
He looked again, and found it was
    A bar of mottled soap.
"A fact so dread," he faintly said,
    "Extinguishes all hope!"

LEWIS CARROLL

THE LETTERS AT SCHOOL

One day the letters went to school,
    And tried to learn each other;
They got so mixed 't was really hard
    To pick out one from t' other.

A went in first, and Z went last;
    The rest all were between them—
K, L, and M, and N, O, P—
    I wish you could have seen them!

B, C, D, E, and J, K, L,
    Soon jostled well their betters;
Q, R, S, T—I grieve to say—
    Were very naughty letters.

Of course, ere long, they came to words—
    What else could be expected?
Till E made D, J, C, and T
    Decidedly dejected.

Now, through it all, the Consonants
    Were rudest and uncouthest,
While all the pretty Vowel girls
    Were certainly the smoothest.

And simple U kept far from Q,
    With face demure and moral,
"Because," she said, "we are, we two,
    So apt to start a quarrel!"

But spiteful P said, "Pooh for U!"
　　(Which made her feel quite bitter),
And, calling O, L, E to help,
　　He really tried to hit her.

Cried A, "Now E and C, come here!
　　If both will aid a minute,
Good P will join in making peace,
　　Or else the mischief's in it."

And smiling E, the ready sprite,
　　Said, "Yes, and count me double."
This done, sweet peace shone o'er the scene,
　　And gone was all the trouble!

Meanwhile, when U and P made up,
　　The Cons'nants looked about them,
And kissed the Vowels, for, you see,
　　They could not do without them.

MARY MAPES DODGE

Mary Mapes Dodge, who wrote this amusing poem, is best-known as the author of Hans Brinker; or The Silver Skates, *a book much loved by children since it was first published more than one hundred years ago. Ms. Dodge was also the first editor of* St. Nicholas, *an extremely popular children's magazine.*

HAVE YOU EVER SEEN?

Have you ever seen a sheet on a river bed?
Or a single hair from a hammer's head?
Has the foot of a mountain any toes?
And is there a pair of garden hose?

Does the needle ever wink its eye?
Why doesn't the wing of a building fly?
Can you tickle the ribs of a parasol?
Or open the trunk of a tree at all?

Are the teeth of a rake ever going to bite?
Have the hands of a clock any left or right?
Can the garden plot be deep and dark?
And what is the sound of the birch's bark?

AUTHOR UNKNOWN

POETRY OF THE EARTH— AND SKY

∾ The snow, the rain, the wind, a rainbow, daffodils, a pear tree in bloom, the sunset, and the moon have all inspired poets. After all, it is these wonders of nature that bring beauty into our lives, affect our moods, even force us to change our plans. In this section some of the world's finest poets celebrate the changing seasons and nature's magic that is everywhere.

Sara Coleridge, who lived in the first half of the nineteenth century, was the daughter of the famous English poet Samuel Taylor Coleridge. She was extremely well read, and was fluent in six languages. She wrote poetry and prose, and after her father's death she edited his papers.

THE MONTHS

January brings the snow,
Makes our feet and fingers glow.

February brings the rain,
Thaws the frozen lake again.

March brings breezes loud and shrill,
Stirs the dancing daffodil.

April brings the primrose sweet,
Scatters daisies at their feet.

May brings flocks of pretty lambs,
Skipping by their fleecy dams.

June brings tulips, lilies, roses,
Fills the children's hands with posies.

Hot July brings cooling showers,
Apricots and gillyflowers.

August brings the sheaves of corn,
Then the harvest home is borne.

Warm September brings the fruit,
Sportsmen then begin to shoot.

Fresh October brings the pheasant,
Then to gather nuts is pleasant.

Dull November brings the blast,
Then the leaves are whirling fast.

Chill December brings the sleet,
Blazing fire and Christmas treat.

SARA COLERIDGE

THE MONTHS

January cold and desolate;
February dripping wet;
March wind ranges;
April changes;
Birds sing in tune
To flowers of May,
And sunny June
Brings longest day;
In scorched July
The storm clouds fly,
Lightning-torn;
August bears corn,
September fruit;
In rough October
Earth must disrobe her;
Stars fall and shoot
In keen November;
And night is long
And cold is strong
In bleak December.

CHRISTINA ROSSETTI

WINTER SONG

Summer joys are o'er
Flowerets bloom no more,
Wintry winds are sweeping;
Through the snowdrifts peeping,
Cheerful evergreen
Rarely now is seen.

Now no plumed throng
Charms the wood with song;
Icebound trees are glittering;
Merry snow birds, twittering,
Fondly strive to cheer
Scenes so cold and drear.

Winter, still see
Many charms in thee,
Love the chilly greeting,
Snowstorms fiercely beating,
And the dear delights
Of the long, long nights.

LUDWIG HOLTY
Translated from the German
by Charles T. Brooks

VELVET SHOES

Let us walk in the white snow
　　In a soundless space;
With footsteps quiet and slow,
　　At a tranquil pace,
　　Under veils of white lace.

I shall go shod in silk,
　　And you in wool,
White as a white cow's milk,
　　More beautiful
　　Than the breast of a gull.

We shall walk through the still town
　　In a windless peace;
We shall step upon white down,
　　Upon silver fleece,
　　Upon softer than these.

We shall walk in velvet shoes:
　　Wherever we go
Silence will fall like dews
　　On white silence below.
　　We shall walk in the snow.

ELINOR WYLIE

Elinor Wylie, who was born in New Jersey and educated in Philadelphia, was a poet, novelist, and an editor. She came from a distinguished family; her father was solicitor general of the United States. Her poetry has a musical quality and her images are always striking. This poem about the snow is one of her loveliest.

THE SNOWFLAKE

Before I melt,
Come, look at me!
This lovely icy filigree!
Of a great forest
In one night
I make a wilderness
Of white:
By skyey cold
Of crystals made,
All softly, on
Your finger laid,
I pause, that you
My beauty see:
Breathe; and I vanish
Instantly.

WALTER DE LA MARE

FEBRUARY TWILIGHT

I stood beside a hill
   Smooth with new-laid snow,
A single star looked out
   From the cold evening glow.

There was no other creature
   That saw what I could see—
I stood and watched the evening star
   As long as it watched me.

SARA TEASDALE

Sara Teasdale was born in St. Louis and educated at home and in private schools. She won a special Pulitzer Prize for Love Songs, a book of poetry. She also wrote poems for children that were collected in two volumes.

WRITTEN IN MARCH

The cock is crowing,
The stream is flowing,
The small birds twitter,
The lake doth glitter,
The green field sleeps in the sun;
The oldest and young
Are at work with the strongest;
The cattle are grazing,
Their heads never raising;
There are forty feeding like one!

Like an army defeated
The snow hath retreated,
And now doth fare ill
On the top of the bare hill;
The ploughboy is whooping—anon—anon—
There's joy in the mountains;
There's life in the fountains;
Small clouds are sailing,
Blue sky prevailing;
The rain is over and gone!

WILLIAM WORDSWORTH

THE MARCH WIND

I come to work as well as play;
　　I'll tell you what I do;
I whistle all the live-long day,
　　"Woo-oo-oo-oo! Woo-oo!"

I toss the branches up and down
　　And shake them to and fro,
I whirl the leaves in flocks of brown,
　　And send them high and low.

I strew the twigs upon the ground,
　　The frozen earth I sweep;
I blow the children round and round
　　And wake the flowers from sleep.

AUTHOR UNKNOWN

WHO HAS SEEN THE WIND?

Who has seen the wind?
　　Neither I nor you:
But when the leaves hang trembling,
　　The wind is passing through.

Who has seen the wind?
　　Neither you nor I:
But when the leaves bow down their heads,
　　The wind is passing by.

CHRISTINA ROSSETTI

THE WIND

I saw you toss the kites on high
And blow the birds about the sky,
And all around I heard you pass,
Like ladies' skirts across the grass—
    O wind, a-blowing all day long,
    O wind, that sings so loud a song!

I saw the different things you did,
But always you yourself you hid.
I felt you push, I heard you call,
I could not see yourself at all—
    O wind, a-blowing all day long,
    O wind, that sings so loud a song!

O you that are so strong and cold,
O blower, are you young or old?
Are you a beast of field and tree,
Or just a stronger child than me?
    O wind, a-blowing all day long,
    O wind, that sings so loud a song!

ROBERT LOUIS STEVENSON

This famous verse
that welcomes the spring is
sung by Pippa, the girl who
works in the silk mill, in
Robert Browning's poetic
drama, Pippa Passes.

PIPPA'S SONG

The year's at the spring
And day's at the morn;
Morning's at seven;
The hillside's dew-pearled;
The lark's on the wing;
The snail's on the thorn:
God's in his heaven—
All's right with the world!

ROBERT BROWNING

SPRING

Sound the flute!
Now it's mute.
Birds delight
Day and night;
Nightingale
In the dale,
Lark in the sky—
Merrily,
Merrily, merrily to welcome in the year.

Little boy,
Full of joy;
Little girl,
Sweet and small;
Cock does crow,
So do you
Merry voice,
Infant noise,
Merrily, merrily, to welcome in the year.

Little lamb,
Here I am;
Come and lick
My white neck;
Let me pull
Your soft wool;
Let me kiss
Your soft face;
Merrily, merrily, we welcome in the year.

WILLIAM BLAKE

THE FOUR SWEET MONTHS

First, April, she with mellow showers
Opens the way for early flowers;
Then after her comes smiling May,
In a more rich and sweet array;
Next enters June, and brings us more
Gems than those two, that went before:
Then, lastly, July comes, and she
More wealth brings in than all those three.

ROBERT HERRICK

APRIL

The roofs are shining from the rain,
 The sparrows twitter as they fly,
And with a windy April grace
 The little clouds go by.

Yet the back-yards are bare and brown
 With only one unchanging tree—
I could not be so sure of spring
 Save that it sings in me.

SARA TEASDALE

APRIL RAIN SONG

Let the rain kiss you.
Let the rain beat upon your head with silver liquid drops.
Let the rain sing you a lullaby.

The rain makes still pools on the sidewalk.
The rain makes running pools in the gutter.
The rain plays a little sleep-song on our roof at night—

And I love the rain.

LANGSTON HUGHES

MAY NIGHT

The spring is fresh and fearless
  And every leaf is new,
The world is brimmed with moonlight,
  The lilac brimmed with dew.

Here in the moving shadows
  I catch my breath and sing—
My heart is fresh and fearless
  And over-brimmed with spring.

SARA TEASDALE

BLOSSOMS

Out of my window I could see
But yesterday, upon the tree,
The blossoms white, like tufts of snow
That had forgotten when to go.

And while I looked out at them, they
Seemed like small butterflies at play,
For in the breeze their flutterings
Made me imagine them with wings.

I must have fancied well, for now
There's not a blossom on the bough,
And out of doors 't is raining fast,
And gusts of wind are whistling past.

With butterflies 't is etiquette
To keep their wings from getting wet,
So, when they knew the storm was near,
They thought it best to disappear.

FRANK DEMPSTER SHERMAN

Frank Dempster Sherman, who was a professor of architecture and graphics at Columbia University, had many of his poems published in St. Nicholas *and other children's magazines.*

Percy Bysshe Shelley, who was only thirty when he died, was one of England's great Romantic poets. He believed that poetry "awakens and enlarges the mind," lifting "the veil from the hidden beauty of the world."

THE CLOUD

I bring fresh showers for the thirsting flowers,
    From the seas and the streams;
I bear light shade for the leaves when laid
    In their noonday dreams.
From my wings are shaken the dews that waken
    The sweet buds every one,
When rocked to rest on their mother's breast,
    As she dances about the sun.
I wield the flail of the lashing hail,
    And whiten the green plains under;
And then again I dissolve it in rain,
    And laugh as I pass in thunder.

PERCY BYSSHE SHELLEY

THE STORM

See lightning is flashing,
The forest is crashing,
The rain will come dashing,
    A flood will be rising anon;

The heavens are scowling,
The thunder is growling,
The loud winds are howling,
    The storm has come suddenly on!

But now the sky clears,
The bright sun appears,
Now nobody fears,
    But soon every cloud will be gone.

SARA COLERIDGE

FOG

The fog comes
on little cat feet.

It sits looking
over harbor and city
on silver haunches
and then moves on.

CARL SANDBURG

THE STORM

There came a wind like a bugle;
It quivered through the grass,
And a green chill upon the heat
So ominous did pass
We barred the windows and the doors
As from an emerald ghost;
The doom's electric moccasin
That very instant passed.
On a strange mob of panting trees,
And fences fled away,
And rivers where the houses ran
The living looked that day.
The bell within the steeple wild
The flying tidings whirled.
How much can come
And much can go,
And yet abide the world!

EMILY DICKINSON

Rain

More than the wind, more than the snow,
More than the sunshine, I love rain;
Whether it droppeth soft and low
Whether it rusheth amain.

Dark as the night it spreadeth its wings,
Slow and silently up on the hills;
Then sweeps o'er the vale, like a steel that springs
From the grasp of a thousand wills.

Swift sweeps under heaven the raven cloud's flight;
And the land and the lakes and the main
Lie belted beneath with steel-bright light,
The light of the swift-rushing rain.

On evening of summer, when sunlight is low,
Soft the rain falls from opal-hued skies;
And the flowers the most delicate summer can show
Are not stirr'd by its gentle surprise.

It falls on the pools, and no wrinkling it makes,
But touching melts in, like the smile
That sinks in the face of a dreamer, but breaks
Not the calm of his dream's happy wile.

The grass rises up as it falls on the meads,
The bird softlier sings in his bower,
And the circles of gnats circle on like wing'd seeds
Through the soft sunny lines of the shower.

Ebenezeer Jones

∾ *David McCord, poet,
editor, critic, and painter,
was born in New York City.
He was on the staff of the
Harvard Alumni Bulletin,
was the drama and music
critic for a Boston news-
paper, and published many
collections of light verse.
He also published a
collection of poems for
children,* One at a Time.

THE RAINBOW

The rainbow arches in the sky,
But in the earth it ends;
But if you ask the reason why,
They'll tell you: "That depends."

It never comes without the rain,
Nor goes without the sun;
But though you try with might and main,
You'll never catch me one,

Perhaps you'll see it once a year,
Perhaps you'll say: "No, twice";
But every time it does appear,
It's very clean and nice.

If I were God, I'd like to win
At sun-and-moon croquet:
I'd drive the rainbow wickets in
Ask someone to play.

DAVID MCCORD

TREES

I think that I shall never see
A poem lovely as a tree.

A tree whose hungry mouth is pressed
Against the earth's sweet flowing breast;

A tree that looks at God all day
And lifts her leafy arms to pray;

A tree that may in summer wear
A nest of robins in her hair;

Upon whose bosom snow has lain;
Who intimately lives with rain.

Poems are made by fools like me,
But only God can make a tree.

JOYCE KILMER

Joyce Kilmer, who was born in New Brunswick, New Jersey, died under German gunfire on July 30, 1918, in the second Battle of the Marne during World War I. This poem, his most popular, first appeared in Poetry *magazine when he was on the staff of* The New York Times Review of Books. *It is said that a white oak tree on the Rutgers University campus inspired the poem which his mother, Annie Kilmer, first set to music.*

TREES

The oak is called the king of trees,
The aspen quivers in the breeze,
The poplar grows up straight and tall,
The peach tree spreads along the wall,
The sycamore gives pleasant shade,
The willow droops in watery glade,
The fir tree useful timber gives,
The beech amid the forest lives.

SARA COLERIDGE

◦ *William Cullen Bryant grew up in Massachusetts. Self-educated, he was for more that fifty years chief editor of the* New York Evening Post. *He was also one of America's earliest and most respected nature writers. He wrote his most famous poem, "Thanatopsis," when he was only seventeen years old.*

THE PLANTING OF THE APPLE TREE

What plant we in this apple tree?
Buds, which the breath of summer days
Shall lengthen into leafy sprays;
Boughs where the thrush, with crimson breast,
Shall haunt and sing and hide her nest;
We plant, upon the sunny lea,
A shadow for the noontide hour,
A shelter from the summer shower,
When we plant the apple tree.

What plant we in this apple tree?
Fruits that shall swell in sunny June,
And redden in the August noon,
And drop, when gentle airs come by,
That fan the blue September sky,
While children come, with cries of glee,
And seek them where the fragrant grass
Betrays their bed to those who pass,
At the foot of the apple tree.

WILLIAM CULLEN BRYANT

PEAR TREE

Silver dust,
lifted from the earth,
higher than my arms reach,
you have mounted,
O, silver,
higher than my arms reach,
you front us with great mass;

no flower ever opened
so staunch a white leaf,
no flower ever parted silver
from such rare silver;

O, white pear,
your flower-tufts
thick on the branch
bring summer and ripe fruits
in their purple hearts.
H. D.

Hilda Doolittle, who wrote as H.D., was born in Bethlehem, Pennsylvania, into a Moravian family. This poem is a good example of her talent for creating lovely imagery with carefully chosen words.

THE DAFFODILS

I wandered lonely as a cloud
That floats on high o'er vales and hills,
When all at once I saw a crowd,
A host, of golden daffodils;
Beside the lake, beneath the trees,
Fluttering and dancing in the breeze.

Continuous as the stars that shine
And twinkle on the milky way,
They stretched in never-ending line
Along the margin of a bay:
Ten thousand saw I at a glance,
Tossing their heads in sprightly dance.

The waves beside them danced; but they
Outdid the sparkling waves in glee:
A poet could not but be gay,
In such a jocund company:
I gazed—and gazed—but little thought
What wealth the show to me had brought:

For oft, when on my couch I lie
In vacant or in pensive mood,
They flash upon that inward eye
Which is the bliss of solitude;
And then my heart with pleasure fills,
And dances with the daffodils.

WILLIAM WORDSWORTH

William Wordsworth was inspired to write this poem after a walk in the woods with his younger sister, Dorothy. She described the scene in her journal: "I never saw daffodils so beautiful. They grew among the mossy stones, about and above them; some rested their head on these stones as on a pillow for weariness; and the rest tossed, and reeled, and danced, and seemed as if they laughed with the wind that blew upon them over the lake. They looked so gay, ever glancing, ever changing."

A SUMMER MORNING

I saw dawn creep across the sky,
And all the gulls go flying by.
I saw the sea put on its dress
Of blue midsummer loveliness,
And heard the trees begin to stir
Green arms of pine and juniper.
I heard the wind call out and say,
"Get up, my dear, it is today!"

RACHEL FIELD

AUGUST

Buttercup nodded and said good-bye.
Clover and daisy went off together,
But the fragrant water lilies lie
Yet moored in the golden August weather.

The swallows chatter about their flight,
The cricket chirps like a rare good fellow,
The asters twinkle in clusters bright,
While the corn grows ripe and the apples mellow.

CELIA THAXTER

BLACKBERRY-PICKING

Late August, given heavy rain and sun
For a full week, the blackberries would ripen.
At first, just one, a glossy purple clot
Among others, red, green, hard as a knot.
You are the first one and its flesh was sweet
Like thickened wine: summer's blood was in it
Leaving stains upon the tongue and lust for
Picking. Then red ones inked up and that hunger
Sent us out with milk-cans, pea-tins, jam-pots
Where briars scratched and wet grass bleached our bones.
Round hayfields, cornfields and potato-drills
We trekked and picked until the cans were full,
Until the tinkling bottoms has been covered
With green ones, and on top big dark blobs burned
Like a plate of eyes. Our hands were peppered
With thorn pricks, our palms sticky as Bluebeard's.

We hoarded the fresh berries in the byre.
But when the bath was filled we found a fur,
A rat-gray fungus, glutting on our cache.
The juice was sticking too. Once off the bush
The fruit fermented, the sweet flesh would turn sour.
I always felt like crying. It wasn't fair
That all the lovely canfuls smelt of rot.
Each year I hoped they'd keep, knew they would not.

SEAMUS HEANEY

SEPTEMBER

The goldenrod is yellow;
    The corn is turning brown;
The trees in apple orchards
    With fruit are bending down.

The gentian's bluest fringes
    Are curling in the sun;
In dusty pods the milkweed
    Its hidden silk has spun.

The sedges flaunt their harvest
    In every meadow nook;
And asters by the brook-side
    Make asters in the brook.

From dewy lanes at morning
    The grapes' sweet odors rise;
At noon the roads all flutter
    With yellow butterflies.

By all these lovely tokens
    September days are here,
With summer's best of weather,
    And autumn's best of cheer.

HELEN HUNT JACKSON

Helen Hunt Jackson was a novelist, poet, and a crusader for the rights of Native Americans. Born in Amherst, Massachusetts, she was a friend and school-mate of Emily Dickinson. After she married she settled in Colorado Springs. She contributed poems to many magazines, wrote travel books, children's books, and the much-admired novel, Ramona.

Carl Sandburg was born in Galesburg, Illinois. His father was a Swedish immigrant who could neither read nor even sign his name. When he was young, Sandburg rode boxcars as a hobo and worked at various jobs as a laborer until he became a journalist. His first book of poems, Chicago, was published when he was thirty-six years old and that was when his career as a poet began.

HARVEST SUNSET

Red gold of pools,
Sunset furrows six o'clock,
And the farmer done in the fields
And the cows in the barns with bulging udders.

Take the cows and the farmer,
Take the barns and bulging udders.
Leave the red gold of pools
And sunset furrows six o'clock.
The farmer's wife is singing.
The farmer's boy is whistling.
I wash my hand in red gold of pools.

CARL SANDBURG

AUTUMN

I love the fitful gust that shakes
    The casement all the day,
And from the mossy elm tree takes
    The faded leaf away,
Twirling it by the window pane
With thousand others down the lane.

I love to see the shaking twig
    Dance till the shut of eve,
The sparrow on the cottage rig
    Whose chirp would make believe
That spring was just now flirting by
In summer's lap with flowers to lie.

I love to see the cottage smoke
    Curl upwards through the naked trees;
The pigeons nestled round the core
    On dull November days like these;
The cock upon the dunghill crowing;
The mill sails on the heath agoing.

The feather from the raven's breast
    Falls on the stubble lea;
The acorns near the old crow's nest
    Fall pattering down the tree.
The grunting pigs that wait for all
Scramble and hurry where they fall.

JOHN CLARE

John Clare was born in a village in Northamptonshire, in England. His father was a thresher, and his mother was a shepherd's daughter, and both of them recited ballads and songs. Clare went to school until he was twelve years old and then began working as a laborer. His first book of verse, Poems Descriptive of Rural Life and Scenery, *was published when he was twenty-seven years old.*

～ Alice Cary was born
on a farm near Cincinnati,
Ohio, the fourth of nine
children. Although they
went to school for only a
few years, she and her sister, Phoebe, published their
first book of poems when
she was thirty. She moved
to New York with her sister
and within six years they
had earned enough money
from their writing to buy a
house. They were both
active in the struggle for
women's rights.

NOVEMBER

The leaves are fading and falling,
    The winds are rough and wild,
The birds have ceased their calling,
    But let me tell you, my child,

Though day by day, as it closes,
    Doth darker and colder grow,
The roots of the bright red roses
    Will keep alive in the snow.

And when the winter is over,
    The boughs will get new leaves,
The quail come back to the clover,
    And the swallow back to the eaves.

The robin will wear on his bosom
    A vest that is bright and new,
And the loveliest wayside blossom
    Will shine with the sun and dew.

The leaves today are whirling,
    The brooks are dry and dumb,
But let me tell you, my darling,
    That spring will be sure to come.

There must be rough, cold weather,
    And winds and rains so wild;
Not all good things together
    Come to us here, my child.

So, when some dear joy loses
    Its beauteous summer glow,
Think how the roots of the roses
    Are kept alive in the snow.

ALICE CARY

I HEARD A BIRD SING

I heard a bird sing
    In the dark of December
A magical thing
    And sweet to remember.

"We are nearer to spring
    Than we were in September,"
I heard a bird sing
    In the dark of December.

OLIVER HERFORD

NATURE

We have neither Summer nor Winter
Neither Autumn nor Spring.
We have instead the days
When the gold sun shines on the lush green canefields—
Magnificently.
The days when the rain beats like bullets on the roofs
And there is no sound but the swish of water in the gullies
And trees struggling in the high Jamaica winds.
Also there are the days when leaves fade from off guango trees
And the reaped canefields lie bare and fallow to the sun.
And best of all there are the days when the mango and the
      logwood blossom
When the bushes are full of the sound of bees and the scent
      of honey,
When the tall grass sways and shivers to the slightest breath
      of air,
When the buttercups have paved the earth with yellow stars
And beauty comes suddenly and the rains have gone.

H. D. CARBERRY

NIGHT STUFF

Listen a while, the moon is a lovely woman, a lonely woman,
    lost in a silver dress, lost in a circus rider's silver dress.

Listen a while, the lake by night is a lonely woman, a lovely
    woman, circled with birches and pines mixing their
    green and white among stars shattered in spray clear nights.

I know the moon and the lake have twisted the roots under
    my heart the same as a lonely woman, a lovely woman,
    in a silver dress, in a circus rider's silver dress.

CARL SANDBURG

Jane Taylor and her sister, Ann, wrote many poems for adults as well as for children. Born in London, Jane wrote this well-known verse in the early nineteenth century. Although many poems about the stars have been written, this is, undoubtedly, the most famous and beloved.

THE STAR

Twinkle, twinkle, little star,
How I wonder what you are!
Up above the world so high,
Like a diamond in the sky.

When the blazing sun is gone,
When he nothing shines upon,
Then you show your little light,
Twinkle, twinkle, all the night.

Then the traveler in the dark,
Thanks you for your tiny spark,
He could not see which way to go
If you did not twinkle so.

In the dark blue sky you keep,
And often through my curtains peep,
For you never shut your eye,
'Til the sun is in the sky.

As your bright and tiny spark
Lights the traveler in the dark—
Though I know not what you are,
Twinkle, twinkle, little star.

JANE TAYLOR

THE MOON'S THE NORTH WIND'S COOKIE

What the Little Girl Said

The Moon's the North Wind's cookie,
He bites it day by day,
Until there's but a rim of scraps
That crumble all away.

The South Wind is a baker
He kneads clouds in his den,
And bakes a crisp new moon that . . . greedy
North . . . Wind . . . eats . . . again!

VACHEL LINDSAY

SILVER

Slowly, silently, now the moon
Walks the night in her silver shoon;
This way, and that, she peers, and sees
Silver fruit upon silver trees;
One by one the casements catch
Her beams beneath the silver thatch;
Couched in his kennel, like a log,
With paws of silver sleeps the dog;
From their shadowy cote the white breasts peep
Of doves in a silver-feathered sleep;
A harvest mouse goes scampering by,
With silver claws, and silver eye;
And moveless fish in the water gleam,
By silver reeds in a silver stream.

WALTER DE LA MARE

POEMS THAT TELL STORIES

Some of the stories in this section are quite long; others are short. A few of them are funny, a couple are mysterious. Some are true stories, others are fables. Many of them are written by famous poets, including Henry Wadsworth Longfellow, Edgar Allen Poe, and Alfred, Lord Tennyson. Several of them, like "A Visit from St. Nicholas" and the story of the Pied Piper may be familiar to you. But all these tales have one thing in common—they are all wonderful poems.

HIAWATHA'S CHILDHOOD

Hiawatha, which means "He Makes Rivers" was a legendary chief of the Onondaga tribe of North American Indians. According to Indian tradition, in the fifteenth century Hiawatha formed the League of Five Nations, known as the Iroquois. Henry Wadsworth Longfellow celebrated his life in a long poem, "The Song of Hiawatha" of which this is the first section. Longfellow wrote the poem in trochaic tetrameters, which capture the rhythm of tom toms.

By the shores of Gitchie Gumee,
By the shining Big-Sea-Water,
Stood the wigwam of Nokimis,
Daughter of the Moon, Nokomis.
Dark behind it rose the forest,
Rose the black and gloomy pine trees,
Rose the firs with cones upon them;
Bright before it beat the water,
Beat the clear and sunny water,
Beat the shining Big-Sea-Water.
    There the wrinkled old Nokomis
Nursed the little Hiawatha,
Rocked him in his linden cradle,
Bedded soft in moss and rushes,
Safely bound with reindeer sinews;
Stilled his fretful wail by saying,
"Hush! the Naked Bear will hear thee!"
Lulled him into slumber, singing,
"Ewa-yea! my little owlet!
Who is this, that lights the wigwam?
With his great eyes lights the wigwam?
Ewa-yea! my little owlet!"
    Many things Nokomis taught him
Of the stars that shine in heaven;
Showed him Ishkoodah, the comet,
Ishkoodah, with fiery tresses;
Showed the Death-Dance of the spirits,
Warriors with their plumes and war clubs,
Flaring far away to northward
In the frosty nights of winter;
Showed the broad white road in heaven,
Pathway of the ghosts, the shadows,
Running straight across the heavens,

Crowded with the ghosts, the shadows.
　　At the door on summer evenings,
Sat the little Hiawatha;
Heard the whispering of the pine trees,
Heard the lapping of the waters,
Sounds of music, words of wonder;
"Minne-wawa!" said the pine trees,
"Mudway-aushka!" said the water.
　　Saw the firefly Wah-wah-taysee,
Flitting through the dusk of evening,
With the twinkle of its candle
Lighting up the brakes and bushes,
And he sang the song of children,
Sang the song Nokomis taught him:
"Wah-wah-taysee, little firefly,
Little, flitting, white-fire insect,
Little, dancing, white-fire creature,
Light me with your little candle,
Ere upon my bed I lay me,
Ere in sleep I close my eyelids!"
　　Saw the moon rise from the water,
Rippling, rounding from the water,
Saw the flecks and shadows on it,
Whispered, "What is that, Nokomis?"
And the good Nokomis answered:
"Once a warrior, very angry,
Seized his grandmother, and threw her
Up into the sky at midnight;
'Tis her body that you see there."
　　Saw the rainbow in the heaven,
In the eastern sky the rainbow,
Whispered, "What is that, Nokomis?"
And the good Nokomis answered:
" 'Tis the heaven of flowers you see there;
All the wild flowers of the forest,

All the lilies of the prairie,
When on earth they fade and perish,
Blossom in that heaven above us."
    When he heard the owls at midnight,
Hooting, laughing in the forest,
"What is that?" he cried in terror;
"What is that," he said, "Nokomis?"
And the good Nokomis answered:
"That is but the owl and owlet,
Talking in their native language,
Talking, scolding at each other."
    Then the little Hiawatha
Learned of every bird its language,
Learned their names and all their secrets,
How they built their nests in summer,
Where they hid themselves in winter,
Talked with them when e'er he met them,
Called them "Hiawatha's Chickens."
Of all beasts he learned the language,
Learned their names and all their secrets,
How the beavers built their lodges,
Where the squirrels hid their acorns,
How the reindeer ran so swiftly,
Why the rabbit was so timid,
Talked with them whene'er he met them,
Called them "Hiawatha's Brothers."

HENRY WADSWORTH LONGFELLOW

AFTER-SCHOOL PRACTICE:
A SHORT STORY

Rain that masks the world
Presses it back too hard against
His forehead at the pane.
Three stories down, umbrellas
Are borne along the current of the sidewalk; a bus
Glides like a giant planchette
In some mysterious pattern through the traffic.
Alone now, he feels lost in the new apartment;
He feels some dark cloud shouldering in.
His wish, if he could have one,
Would be for the baby next door to cry out
This minute, signifying end of nap.
Then he could practice. (Apartment life
Is full of these considerations.)
But when finally this does happen,
He still for a time postpones the first chord.
He looks around, full of secrets;
His strange deep thoughts have brought, so far, no harm.
Carefully, with fists and elbows, he prepares
One dark, tremendous chord
Never heard before—his own thunder!
And strikes.
        And the strings will quiver with it
A long time before the held pedal
Gives up the sound completely—this throbbing
Of the piano's great exposed heart.
Then, soberly, he begins his scales.

And gradually the storm outside dies away also.

DONALD JUSTICE

CASEY AT THE BAT

The outlook wasn't brilliant for the Mudville nine that day;
The score stood four to two with but one inning more to play.
And then when Cooney died at first, and Barrows did the same,
A sickly silence fell upon the patrons of the game.

A straggling few got up to go in deep despair. The rest
Clung to that hope which springs eternal in the human breast;
They thought if only Casey could but get a whack at that—
We'd put up even money now with Casey at the bat.

But Flynn preceded Casey, as did also Jimmy Blake,
And the former was a lulu and the latter was a cake;
So upon that stricken multitude grim melancholy sat,
For there seemed but little chance of Casey's getting to the bat.

But Flynn let drive a single, to the wonderment of all,
And Blake, the much despis-ed, tore the cover off the ball;
And when the dust had lifted, and the men saw what had occurred,
There was Johnnie safe at second and Flynn a-hugging third.

Then from five thousand throats and more there rose a lusty yell;
It rumbled through the valley, it rattled in the dell;
It knocked upon the mountain and recoiled upon the flat,
For Casey, mighty Casey, was advancing to the bat.

There was ease in Casey's manner as he stepped into his place;
There was pride in Casey's bearing and a smile on Casey's face.
And when, responding to the cheers, he lightly doffed his hat,
No stranger in the crowd could doubt 'twas Casey at the bat.

Ten thousand eyes were on him as he rubbed his hands with dirt;
Five thousand tongues applauded when he wiped them on his shirt.
Then while the writhing pitcher ground the ball into his hip,
Defiance gleamed in Casey's eye, a sneer curled Casey's lip.

And now the leather-covered sphere came hurtling through the air,
And Casey stood a-watching it in haughty grandeur there.
Close by the sturdy batsman the ball unheeded sped—
"That ain't my style," said Casey. "Strike one," the umpire said.

From the benches, black with people, there went up a muffled roar,
Like the beating of the storm-waves on a stern and distant shore.
"Kill him! Kill the umpire!" shouted someone on the stand;
And it's likely they'd have killed him had not Casey raised his hand.

With a smile of Christian charity great Casey's visage shone;
He stilled the rising tumult; he bade the game go on;
He signaled to the pitcher, and once more the spheroid flew;
But Casey still ignored it, and the umpire said, "Strike two."

"Fraud!" cried the maddened thousands, and echo answered fraud;
But one scornful look from Casey and the audience was awed.
They saw his face grow stern and cold, they saw his muscles strain,
And they knew that Casey wouldn't let that ball go by again.

The sneer is gone from Casey's lip, his teeth are clenched in hate;
He pounds with cruel violence his bat upon the plate.
And now the pitcher holds the ball, and now he lets it go,
And now the air is shattered by the force of Casey's blow.

Oh, somewhere in this favored land the sun is shining bright;
The band is playing somewhere, and somewhere hearts are light,
And somewhere men are laughing, and somewhere children shout;
But there is no joy in Mudville—mighty Casey has struck out.

ERNEST LAWRENCE THAYER

This is certainly the greatest poem about baseball that has ever been written. There have even been several film versions. Its author, Ernest Lawrence Thayer, had a humor column in a San Francisco newspaper and it was in that column, on Sunday, June 3, 1988, that Casey first appeared.

THE SONG OF THE WANDERING AENGUS

I went out to the hazel wood,
Because a fire was in my head,
And cut and peeled a hazel wand,
And hooked a berry to a thread;
And when white moths were on the wing,
And moth-like stars were flickering out,
I dropped the berry in a stream
And caught a little silver trout.

When I had laid it on the floor
I went to blow the fire aflame,
But something rustled on the floor,
And someone called me by my name:
It had become a glimmering girl
With apple blossom in her hair
Who called me by my name and ran
And faded through the brightening air.

Though I am old and wandering
Through hollow lands and hilly lands,
I will find out where she has gone,
And kiss her lips and take her hands;
And walk among long dappled grass,
And pluck till time and times are done
The silver apples of the moon,
The golden apples of the sun.

WILLIAM BUTLER YEATS

The great Irish poet William Butler Yeats was inspired to write this poem by a story told to him by an old man: "One time I was cutting timber over in Inchy, and about eight o'clock one morning, when I got there, I saw a girl picking nuts, with her hair hanging down over her shoulders; brown hair; and she had a good clean face, and she was tall, and nothing on her head, and her dress no way gaudy, but simple. And when she felt me coming, she gathered herself up, and was gone, as if the earth had swallowed her up. And I followed her, and looked for her, but I never could see her again from that day to this, never again."

PAUL REVERE'S RIDE

Listen, my children, and you shall hear
Of the midnight ride of Paul Revere,
On the eighteenth of April, in Seventy-five;
Hardly a man is now alive
Who remembers that famous day and year.

He said to his friend, "If the British march
By land or sea from the town tonight,
Hang a lantern aloft in the belfry arch
Of the North Church tower as a signal light—
One, if by land, and two, if by sea;
And I on the opposite shore will be,
Ready to ride and spread the alarm
Through every Middlesex village and farm,
For the country folk to be up and to arm."
Then he said, "Good night" and with muffled oar
Silently rowed to the Charlestown shore,
Just as the moon rose over the bay,
Where swinging wide at her moorings lay
The *Somerset*, British man-of-war;
A phantom ship, with each mast and spar
Across the moon like a prison bar,
And a huge black hulk, that was magnified
By its own reflection in the tide.
Meanwhile, his friend, through alley and street,
Wanders and watches, with eager ears,
Till in the silence around him he hears
The muster of men at the barrack door,
The sound of arms, and the tramp of feet,
And the measured tread of the grenadiers,
Marching down to their boats on the shore.

Paul Revere, a silver-smith and an engraver, was one of many couriers working for the rebels during the American Revolution. Although the poem is inaccurate in some of the historical details, Revere did make his ride on April 18, 1775. It would not have been remembered if Henry Wadsworth Longfellow had not written about it.

Then he climbed to the tower of the Old North Church,
By the wooden stairs, with stealthy tread,
To the belfry-chamber overhead,
And startled the pigeons from their perch
On the somber rafters, that round him made
Masses and moving shapes of shade—
By the trembling ladder, steep and tall,
To the highest window in the wall,
Where he paused to listen and look down
A moment on the roofs of the town,
And the moonlight flowing over all.
Beneath, in the churchyard, lay the dead,
In their night-encampment on the hill,
Wrapped in silence so deep and still
That he could hear, like a sentinel's tread,
The watchful night wind, as it went
Creeping along from tent to tent,
And seeming to whisper, "All is well!"
A moment only he feels the spell
Of the place and the hour, and the secret dread
Of the lonely belfry and the dead;
For suddenly all his thoughts are bent
On a shadowy something far away,
Where the river widens to meet the bay—
A line of black that bends and floats
On the rising tide, like a bridge of boats.

Meanwhile, impatient to mount and ride,
Booted and spurred, with a heavy stride
On the opposite shore walked Paul Revere.
Now he patted his horse's side,
Now gazed at the landscape far and near,
Then, impetuous, stamped the earth,
And turned and tightened his saddle girth;
But mostly he watched with eager search
The belfry tower of the Old North Church,

As it rose above the graves on the hill,
Lonely and spectral and somber and still.
And lo! as he looks, on the belfry's height
A glimmer, and then a gleam of light!
He springs to the saddle, the bridle he turns,
But lingers and gazes, till full on his sight
A second lamp in the belfry burns!
A hurry of hoofs in a village street,
A shape in the moonlight, a bulk in the dark,
And beneath, from the pebbles, in passing, a spark
Struck out by a steed flying fearless and fleet:
That was all! And yet, through the gloom and the light,
The fate of a nation was riding that night;
And the spark struck out by that steed, in his flight,
Kindled the land into flame with its heat.
He has left the village and mounted the steep,
And beneath him, tranquil and broad and deep,
Is the Mystic, meeting the ocean tides;
And under the alders that skirt its edge,
Now soft on the sand, now loud on the ledge,
Is heard the tramp of his steed as he rides.

It was twelve by the village clock,
When he crossed the bridge into Medford town.
He heard the crowing of the cock,
And the barking of the farmer's dog,
And felt the damp of the river fog,
That rises after the sun goes down.
It was one by the village clock,
When he galloped into Lexington.
He saw the gilded weathercock
Swim in the moonlight as he passed,
And the meeting-house windows, blank and bare,
Gaze at him with a spectral glare,
As if they already stood aghast
At the bloody work they would look upon.

It was two by the village clock,
When he came to the bridge in Concord town.
He heard the bleating of the flock,
And the twitter of birds among the trees,
And felt the breath of the morning breeze
Blowing over the meadows brown.
And one was safe and asleep in his bed
Who at the bridge would be first to fall,
Who that day would be lying dead,
Pierced by a British musket-ball.

You know the rest. In the books you have read
How the British Regulars fired and fled—
How the farmers gave them ball for ball,
From behind each fence and farmyard wall,
Chasing the redcoats down the lane,
Then crossing the fields to emerge again
Under the trees at the turn of the road,
And only pausing to fire and load.

So through the night rode Paul Revere;
And so through the night went his cry of alarm
To every Middlesex village and farm—
A cry of defiance and not of fear,
A voice in the darkness, a knock at the door,
And a word that shall echo forevermore!
For, borne on the night wind of the Past,
Through all our history, to the last,
In the hour of darkness and peril and need,
The people will awaken and listen to hear
The hurrying hoofbeats of that steed,
And the midnight message of Paul Revere.

HENRY WADSWORTH LONGFELLOW

MILLER'S END

When we moved to Miller's End,
    Every afternoon at four
A thin shadow of a shade
    Quavered through the garden door.

Dressed in black from top to toe
    And in a veil about her head.
To us it seemed as though
    She came walking from the dead.

With a basket on her arm
    Through the hedge-gap she would pass,
Never a mark that we could spy
    On the flagstones or the grass.

When we told the garden boy
    How we saw the phantom glide,
With a grin his face was bright
    As the pool he stood beside.

"That's no ghost-walk," Billy said
    "Nor a ghost you fear to stop—
Only old Miss Wickerby
    On a short cut to the shop."

So next day we lay in wait,
    Passed a civil time of day,
Said how pleased we were she came
    Daily down our garden way.

Suddenly her cheek it paled,
    Turned, as quick, from ice to flame.
"Tell me," said Miss Wickerby,
"Who spoke of me, and my name?"

"Bill the garden boy." She sighed,
    Said, "Of course you could not know
How he drowned—that very pool,
    A frozen winter,—long ago."

CHARLES CAUSLEY

Charles Causley was born in Cornwall, England, where he was educated and where he returned, after serving in the Royal Navy for six years during World War Two, and became a teacher. He has written many poems and stories for children, as well as poetry for adults.

THE SPIDER AND THE FLY

A Fable

"Will you walk into my parlor?" said the spider to the fly;
" 'Tis the prettiest little parlor that ever you did spy.
The way into my parlor is up a winding stair,
And I have many pretty things to show when you are there."

"O no, no," said the little fly, "to ask me is in vain
"For who goes up your winding stair can ne'er come down again."

"I'm sure you must be weary, dear, with soaring up so high;
Will you rest upon my little bed?" said the spider to the fly.
"There are pretty curtains drawn around, the sheets are fine
      and thin,
And if you like to rest awhile, I'll snugly tuck you in."

"O no, no," said the little fly, "for I've often heard it said,
They never, never wake again, who sleep upon your bed."

Said the cunning spider to the fly, "Dear friend, what shall I do,
To prove the warm affection I've always felt for you?
I have within my pantry good store of all that's nice;
I'm sure you're very welcome; will you please to take a slice?"

"O no, no," said the little fly, "kind sir, that cannot be;
I've heard what's in your pantry, and I do not wish to see."

"Sweet creature!" said the spider, "you're witty and you're wise.
How handsome are your gauzy wings, how brilliant are your eyes!
I have a little looking-glass upon my parlor shelf,
If you'll step in one moment, dear, you shall behold yourself."

"I thank you, gentle sir," she said, "for what you're pleased to say,
And bidding you good morning soon, I'll call another day,"

The spider turned him round about, and went into his den,
For well he knew the silly fly would soon be back again:
So he wove a subtle web, in a little corner sly,
And set his table ready to dine upon the fly.
Then he came out to his door again, and merrily did sing,
"Come hither, hither, pretty fly, with the pearl and silver wing:
Your robes are green and purple; there's a crest upon your head;
Your eyes are like the diamond bright, but mine are dull as lead."

Alas, alas! how very soon this silly little fly,
Hearing his wily flattering words, came slowly flitting by.
With buzzing wings she hung aloft, then near and nearer drew,
Thinking only of her brilliant eyes, and green and purple hue;
Thinking only of her crested head—poor foolish thing! At last,
Up jumped the cunning spider, and fiercely held her fast.
He dragged her up his winding stair, into his dismal den,
Within his little parlor; but she ne'er came out again!

And now, dear little children, who may this story read,
To idle, silly, flattering words, I pray you ne'er give heed;
Unto an evil counselor close heart, and ear, and eye,
And take a lesson from this tale of the spider and the fly.

MARY HOWITT

THE CHARGE OF THE LIGHT BRIGADE

I

Half a league, half a league
    Half a league onward,
All in the valley of Death
    Rode the six hundred.
"Forward, the Light Brigade!
Charge for the guns!" he said:
Into the valley of Death
    Rode the six hundred.

II

"Forward, the Light Brigade!"
Was there a man dismay'd?
Not tho' the soldier knew
    Someone had blunder'd:
Their's not to make reply,
Their's not to reason why,
Their's but to do and die:
Into the valley of Death
    Rode the six hundred.

III

Cannon to right of them,
Cannon to left of them,
Cannon in front of them
    Volley'd and thunder'd;
Storm'd at with shot and shell,
Boldly they rode and well,
Into the jaws of Death,
Into the mouth of Hell
    Rode the six hundred.

IV

Flash'd all their sabres bare,
Flash'd as they turn'd in air
Sabring the gunners there,
Charging an army, while
    All the world wonder'd:
Plunged in the battery smoke
Right thro' the line they broke;
Cossack and Russian
Reel'd from the sabre stroke
    Shatter'd and sunder'd.
Then they rode back, but not—
    Not the six hundred.

V

Cannon to right of them,
Cannon to left of them,
Cannon behind them
    Volley'd and thunder'd;
Storm'd at with shot and shell,
While horse and hero fell,
They that had fought so well
Came thro' the jaws of Death,
Back from the mouth of Hell,
All that was left of them,
    Left of six hundred.

VI

When can their glory fade?
O the wild charge they made!
    All the world wonder'd.
Honor the charge they made!
Honor the Light Brigade,
    Noble six hundred!

ALFRED, LORD TENNYSON

During the Crimean War, fought by Britain against Russia, the Charge of the Light Brigade took place on October 25, 1854. Two hundred and forty-seven men out of six hundred and thirty-seven were killed or wounded because one of the British officers misunderstood an order. Tennyson composed this poem in a few minutes, after reading about the battle in the newspaper. In the article there was the phrase "some one had blundered," and this set the meter for the poem.

THE RAVEN

Once upon a midnight dreary, while I pondered, weak and weary,
    Over many a quaint and curious volume of forgotten lore,
While I nodded, nearly napping, suddenly there came a tapping,
    As of someone gently rapping, rapping at my chamber door.
    " 'Tis some visitor," I muttered, "tapping at my chamber door;
        Only this, and nothing more."

Ah, distinctly I remember, it was in the bleak December,
    And each separate dying ember wrought its ghost upon the floor.
Eagerly I wished the morrow; vainly I had sought to borrow
    From my books surcease of sorrow, sorrow for the lost Lenore,
    For the rare and radiant maiden whom the angels name Lenore,
        Nameless here forevermore.

And the silken and uncertain rustling of each purple curtain
    Thrilled me—filled me with fantastic terrors never felt before;
So that now, to still the beating of my heart, I stood repeating,
    " 'Tis some visitor entreating entrance at my chamber door,
    Some late visitor entreating entrance at my chamber door;
        This it is, and nothing more."

Presently my soul grew stronger; hesitating then no longer,
    "Sir," said I, "or madam, truly your forgiveness I implore;
But the fact is, I was napping, and so gently you came rapping,
    And so faintly you came tapping, tapping at my chamber door,
    That I scarce was sure I heard you." Here I opened wide the door;
        Darkness there, and nothing more.

Deep into the darkness peering, long I stood there, wondering, fearing,
    Doubting, dreaming dreams no mortals ever dared to dream before;
But the silence was unbroken, and the stillness gave no token,
    And the only word there spoken was the whispered word, "Lenore?"
    This I whispered, and an echo murmured back the word, "Lenore!"
        Merely this, and nothing more.

Back into the chamber turning, all my soul within me burning,
    Soon again I heard a tapping, something louder than before,
"Surely," said I, "surely, that is something at my window lattice;
    Let me see, then, what thereat is, and this mystery explore;
    Let my heart be still a moment, and this mystery explore;
        'Tis the wind, and nothing more."

Open here I flung the shutter, when, with many a flirt and flutter,
    In there stepped a stately raven, of the saintly days of yore.
Not the least obeisance made he; not a minute stopped or stayed he;
    But with mein of lord or lady, perched above my chamber door;
    Perched upon a bust of Pallas, just above my chamber door,
        Perched, and sat, and nothing more.

Then this ebony bird beguiling my sad fancy into smiling,
    By the grave and stern decorum of the countenance it wore,
"Though thy crest be shorn and shaven, thou," I said, "art sure
        no craven,
    Ghastly, grim, and ancient raven, wandering from the nightly shore,
    Tell me what they lordly name is on the Night's Plutonian shore."
        Quoth the raven, "Nevermore."

Much I marvelled this ungainly fowl to hear discourse so plainly,
    Though its answer little meaning, little relevancy bore;
For we cannot help agreeing that no living human being
    Ever yet was blessed with seeing bird above his chamber door,
    Bird or beast upon the sculptured bust above his chamber door,
        With such name as "Nevermore."

But the raven, sitting lonely on that placid bust, spoke only
    That one word, as if his soul in that one word he did outpour,
Nothing further then he uttered; not a feather then he fluttered;
    Till I scarcely more than muttered, "Other friends have flown
        before;
    On the morrow he will leave me, as my hopes have flown
        before."
        Then the bird said, "Nevermore."

Edgar Allan Poe was born in Boston, the child of travelling actors. He was orphaned when he was two years old and raised in Virginia. Although Poe lived only to the age of forty, in his short life he was an influential maga-zazine editor and the first author of horror tales, science fiction stories, and detective mysteries. "The Raven" is probably his most famous poems. He rewrote it many times; at first he intended his mysterious bird to be an owl.

Startled at the stillness broken by reply so aptly spoken,
    "Doubtless," said I, "what it utters is its only stock and store,
Caught from some unhappy master, whom unmerciful disaster
    Followed fast and followed faster, till his songs one burden bore,
    Till the dirges of his hope that melancholy burden bore
            Of "Never—nevermore."

But the raven still beguiling all my fancy into smiling,
    Straight I wheeled a cushioned seat in front of bird and
            bust and door;
Then, upon the velvet sinking, I betook myself to linking
    Fancy unto fancy, thinking what this ominous bird of yore,
    What this grim, ungainly, ghastly, gaunt, and ominous bird
        of yore
            Meant in croaking, "Nevermore."

This I sat engaged in guessing, but no syllable expressing
    To the fowl whose fiery eyes now burned into my bosom's core;
This and more I sat divining, with my head at ease reclining
    On the cushion's velvet lining that the lamplight gloated o'er,
    But whose velvet-violet lining with the lamplight gloating o'er,
            She shall press, ah, nevermore!

Then, methought, the air grew denser, perfumed from an unseen
        censer
    Swung by seraphim whose footfalls tinkled on the tufted floor.
"Wretch," I cried, "thy God hath lent thee—by these angels he
        hath sent thee
    Respite—respite and nepenthe from thy memories of Lenore;
    Quaff, oh quaff this kind nepenthe and forget this lost Lenore!"
            Quoth the Raven, "Nevermore."

"Prophet!" said I, "think of evil!—prophet still, if bird or devil!—
    Whether Tempter sent, or whether tempest tossed thee
        here ashore,
Desolate yet all undaunted, on this desert land enchanted—
    On this home by Horror haunted—tell me truly, I implore—
    Is there—is there balm in Gilead?—tell me—tell me, I implore!"
        Quoth the Raven, "Nevermore."

"Prophet!" said I, "thing of evil!—prophet still, if bird or devil!
    By that Heaven that bends above us—by that God we
        both adore—
Tell this soul with sorrow laden if, within the distant Aidenn,
    It shall clasp a sainted maiden whom the angels name Lenore—
    Clasp a rare and radiant maiden whom the angels name Lenore."
        Quoth the Raven, "Nevermore."

"Be that word our sign of parting, bird or fiend!" I shrieked, upstarting—
    "Get thee back into the tempest and the Night's Plutonian
        shore!
Leave no black plume as a token of that lie thy soul hath spoken!
    Leave my loneliness unbroken!—quit the bust above my door!
    Take thy beak from out my heart, and take thy form from
        off my door!"
        Quoth the Raven, "Nevermore."

And the Raven, never flitting, still is sitting, still is sitting
    On the pallid bust of Pallas just above my chamber door;
And his eyes have all the seeming of a demon's that is dreaming,
    And the lamplight o'er him streaming throws his shadow
        on the floor;
    And my soul from out that shadow that lies floating on the floor
        Shall be lifted—nevermore!

EDGAR ALLAN POE

MATILDA WHO TOLD LIES, AND WAS BURNED TO DEATH

Matilda told such dreadful lies,
It made one gasp and stretch one's eyes;
Her Aunt, who, from her earliest youth,
Had kept a strict regard for truth,
Attempted to believe Matilda:
The effort very nearly killed her,
And would have done so, had not she
Discovered this infirmity.
For once, toward the close of day,
Matilda, growing tired of play,
And finding she was left alone,
Went tiptoe to the telephone
And summoned the immediate aid
Of London's noble fire brigade.
Within an hour the gallant band
Were pouring in on every hand,
From Putney, Hackney Downs, and Bow
With courage high and hearts a-glow
They galloped, roaring through the town,
"Matilda's house is burning down!"
Inspired by British cheers and loud
Proceeding from the frenzied crowd,
They ran their ladders through a score
Of windows on the ballroom floor;
And took peculiar pains to souse
The pictures up and down the house,
Until Matilda's Aunt succeeded
In showing them they were not needed;
And even then she had to pay
To get the men to go away!
It happened that a few weeks later
Her Aunt was off to the theater

To see that interesting play
The Second Mrs. Tanqueray,
She had refused to take her niece
To hear this entertaining piece:
A deprivation just and wise
To punish her for telling lies.
That night a fire did break out—
You should have heard Matilda shout!
You should have heard her scream and bawl,
And throw the window up and call
To people passing in the street—
(The rapidly increasing heat
Encouraging her to obtain
Their confidence)—but all in vain!
For every time she shouted "Fire!"
They only answered "Little liar!"
And therefore when her Aunt returned,
Matilda, and the house, were burned.

HILAIRE BELLOC

This gruesome story is from Hilaire Belloc's book Cautionary Tales, *which has been extremely popular with children since he wrote it more than one hundred years ago.*

CASABIANCA

The boy stood on the burning deck,
    Whence all but he had fled;
The flame that lit the battle's wreck,
    Shone round him o'er the dead;
Yet beautiful and bright he stood
    As born to rule the storm!
A creature of heroic blood,
    A proud, though childlike form!

The flames roll'd on—he would not go
    Without his father's word;
That father, faint in death below,
    His voice no longer heard.
He call'd aloud: "Say, Father, say
    If yet my task is done!"
He knew not that the chieftain lay
    Unconscious of his son.

"Speak, Father!" once again he cried,
    "If I may yet be gone!"
And but the booming shots replied,
    And fast the flames roll'd on.
Upon his brow he felt their breath,
    And in his waving hair;
And look'd from that lone post of death
    In still, yet brave, despair;

And shouted but once more aloud,
    "My father! must I stay?"
While o'er him fast through sail and shroud,
    The wreathing fires made way.
They wrapt the ship in splendor wild,
    They caught the flag on high,
And stream'd above the gallant child
    Like banners in the sky.

There came a burst of thunder sound—
    The boy—O! where was he?
Ask of the winds that far around
    With fragments strewed the sea,
With mast, and helm, and pennon fair,
    That well had borne their part;
But the noblest thing which perish'd there
    Was that young faithful heart!

FELICIA DOROTHEA HEMANS

This poem memorializes an actual event. During the Battle of the Nile, Louis de Casabianca was the commander of the French ship Orient. His thirteen-year-old son remained on deck after the ship caught fire and died when the ship's powder exploded. Felicia Hemans, whose first of many books of poems was published when she was fifteen years old, wrote this poem in 1829.

A Visit from Mr. Fox

The fox set out in hungry plight,
    And begged the moon to give him light,
For he'd many a mile to travel that night,
    Before he could reach his den, Oh!

First he came to a farmer's yard,
    Where the ducks and geese declared it was hard
That their nerves should be shaken, and their rest be marred
    By a visit from Mr. Fox, Oh!

He seized the gray goose by the sleeve,
    Says he, "Madame Gray Goose, by your leave,
I'll carry you off without reprieve,
    And take you away to my den, Oh!"

He seized the gray duck by the neck,
    And flung her over across his back,
While the old duck cried out, "Quack, quack, quack!"
    With her legs dangling down behind, Oh!

Then old Mrs. Flipper Flapper jumped out of her bed,
    And out of the window she popped her head,
Crying, "John, John, John, the gray goose is gone,
    And the fox is off to his den, Oh!"

So the fox he hurried home to his den,
    To his dear little foxes eight, nine, ten.
"We're in luck, here's a big, fat duck
    With her legs dangling down behind, Oh!"

The fox sat down with his hungry wife,
    And they made a good meal without fork or knife.
They never had a better time in all their life,
    And the little ones picked the bones, Oh!

AUTHOR UNKNOWN

THE PIED PIPER OF HAMELIN

A Child's Story

I

Hamelin Town's in Brunswick,
    By famous Hanover City;
The river Weser, deep and wide,
Washes its wall on the southern side;
A pleasanter spot you never spied;
    But, when begins my ditty,
Almost five hundred years ago,
To see the townsfolk suffer so
    From vermin, was a pity.

II

    Rats!
They fought the dogs and killed the cats,
    And bit the babies in the cradles,
And ate the cheeses out of the vats,
    And licked the soup from the cooks' own ladles,
Split open the kegs of salted sprats,
Made nests inside men's Sunday hats,
And even spoiled the women's chats
    By drowning their speaking
    With shrieking and squeaking
In fifty different sharps and flats.

III

At last the people in a body
    To the Town Hall came flocking:
" 'Tis clear," cried they, "our Mayor's a noddy;
    And as for our Corporation—shocking
To think we buy gowns lined with ermine
For dolts that can't or won't determine
What's best to rid us of our vermin!

Robert Browning was brought up with his only sister, Sarianna, in Camberwell in southeast London. His father, who worked for the Bank of England, had a library of more than six thousand books and it was here that Browning got most of his education. He wrote his first volume of poems when he was twelve years old, but his first published poem did not appear until nine years later. He dedicated this poem about the Pied Piper to "W.H. THE YOUNGER," who he addresses as "Willy" in the last stanza.

You hope, because you're old and obese,
To find in the furry civic robe ease?
Rouse up, sirs! Give your brains a racking
To find the remedy we're lacking.
Or, sure as fate, we'll send you packing!"
At this the Mayor and corporation
Quaked with a might consternation.

IV

An hour they sat in council,
        At length the Mayor broke silence:
"For a guilder I'd my ermine gown sell,
        I wish I were a mile hence!
It's easy to bid one rack one's brain—
I'm sure my poor head aches again,
I've scratched it so, and all in vain.
Oh for a trap, a trap, a trap!"
Just as he said this, what should hap
At the chamber door but a gentle tap?
"Bless us," cried the Mayor, "what's this?"
(With the Corporation as he sat,
Looking little though wondrous fat;
Nor brighter was his eye, nor moister
Than a too-long-opened oyster,
Save when at noon his paunch grew mutinous
For a plate of turtle green and glutinous)
"Only a scraping of shoes on the mat?
Anything like the sound of a rat
Makes my heart go pit-a-pat!"

V

"Come in!"—the Mayor cried, looking bigger:
And in did come the strangest figure!
His queer long coat from heel to head
Was half of yellow and half of red.

And he himself was tall and thin,
With sharp blue eyes, each like a pin,
With light loose hair, yet swarthy skin,
No tuft on cheek nor beard on chin.
But lips where smiles went out and in;
There was no guessing his kith and kin:
And nobody could enough admire
The tall man and his quaint attire.
Quoth one: "It's as my great-grandsire,
Starting up at the Trump of Doom's tone,
Had walked this way from his painted tombstone!"

VI

He advanced to the council table:
And, "Please your honors," said he, "I'm able,
By means of a secret charm, to draw
    All creatures living beneath the sun,
    That creep or swim or fly or run,
After me so as you never saw!
And I chiefly use my charm
On creatures that do people harm,
The mole and toad and newt and viper;
And people call me the Pied Piper."
(And here they noticed round his neck
    A scarf of red and yellow stripe,
To match with his coat of the selfsame check;
    And at the scarf's end a pipe;
And his fingers, they noticed, were ever straying
As if impatient to be playing
Upon this pipe, as low it dangled
Over his vesture so old-fangled.)
"Yet," said he, "poor piper as I am,
In Tartary I freed the Cham,
    Last June, from his huge swarms of gnats;
I eased in Asia the Nizam
    Of a monstrous brood of vampire bats;

And as for what your brain bewilders,
    If I can rid your town of rats
Will you give me a thousand guilders?"
"One? Fifty thousand!"—was the exclamation
Of the astonished Mayor and Corporation.

VII

Into the street the Piper stepped,
    Smiling first a little smile,
As if he knew what magic slept
    In his quiet pipe the while.
Then, like a musical adept,
To blow the pipe his lips he wrinkled,
And green and blue his sharp eyes twinkled,
Like a candle flame where salt is sprinkled;
And ere three shrill notes the pipe uttered,
You heard as if an army muttered;
And the muttering grew to a grumbling;
And the grumbling grew to a mighty rumbling;
And out of the houses the rats came tumbling.
Great rats, small rats, lean rats, brawny rats,
Brown rats, black rats, gray rats, tawny rats,
Grave old plodders, gay young friskers,
    Fathers, mothers, uncles, cousins,
Cocking tails and pricking whiskers,
    Families by tens and dozens,
Brothers, sisters, husbands, wives—
Followed the Piper for their lives.
From street to street he piped advancing,
And step for step they followed dancing,
Until they came to the river Weser,
    Wherein all plunged and perished!
—Save one who, stout as Julius Caesar,

Swam across and lived to carry

 (As he, the manuscript he cherished)

To Rat-land home his commentary:

Which was, "At the first shrill notes of the pipe,

I heard a sound as of scraping tripe,

And putting apples, wondrous ripe,

Into a cider press's gripe:

And a moving away of pickle tub-boards,

And a leaving ajar of conserve cupboards,

And a drawing the corks of train-oil flasks,

And a breaking the hoops of butter casks:

And it seemed as if a voice

 (Sweeter far than by harp or by psaltery

Is breathed) called out, "Oh rats, rejoice!

 The world is grown to one vast drysaltery!

So munch on, crunch one, take your nuncheon,

Breakfast, supper, dinner, luncheon!"

And just as a bulky sugar-puncheon,

All ready staved, like a great sun shone

Glorious scarce an inch before me,

Just as methought it said, "Come, bore me!"

—I found the Weser rolling o'er me."

VIII

You should have heard the Hamelin people

Ringing the bells till they rocked the steeple.

"Go," cried the Mayor, "and get long poles,

Poke out the nests and block up the holes!

Consult with carpenters and builders,

And leave in our town not even a trace

Of the rats!"—when suddenly, up the face

Of the Piper perked in the marketplace,

With a "First, if you please, my thousand guilders!"

IX

A thousand guilders! The Mayor looked blue;
So did the Corporation, too.
For council dinners made rare havoc
With Claret, Moselle, Vin-de-Grave, Hock;
And half the money would replenish
Their cellar's biggest butt with Rhenish.
To pay this sum to a wandering fellow
With a gypsy coat of red and yellow!
"Beside," quoth the Mayor with a knowing wink,
"Our business was done at the river's brink;
We saw with our eyes the vermin sink,
And what's dead can't come to life, I think.
So, friend, we're not the folks to shrink
From the duty of giving you something for drink,
And a matter of money to put in your poke;
But as for the guilders, what we spoke
Of them, as you very well know, was in joke.
Beside, our losses have made us thrifty.
A thousand guilders! Come, take fifty!"

X

The Piper's face fell, and he cried
"No trifling! I can't wait, beside!
I've promised to visit by dinner time
Baghdad, and accept the prime
Of the head cook's pottage, all he's rich in,
For having left, in the Caliph's kitchen,
Of a nest of scorpions no survivor:
With him I proved no bargain-driver.
With you don't think I'll bate a stiver!
And folks who put me in a passion
May find me pipe after another fashion."

XI

"How?" cried the Mayor, "d'ye think I brook
Being worse treated than a Cook?
Insulted by a lazy ribald
With idle pipe and vesture piebald?
You threaten us, fellow? Do your worst,
Blow your pipe there till you burst!"

XII

Once more he stepped into the street
    And to his lips again
    Laid his long pipe of smooth straight cane;
And ere he blew three notes (such sweet
Soft notes as yet musician's cunning
    Never gave the enraptured air)
There was a rustling that seemed like a bustling
Of merry crowds jostling and pitching and hustling,
Small feet were pattering, wooden shoes clattering,
Little hands clapping and little tongues chattering,
And, like the fowls in a farmyard when barley is scattering,
Out came the children running.
All the little boys and girls,
With rose cheeks and flaxen curls,
And sparkling eyes and teeth like pearls,
Tripping and skipping, ran merrily after
The wonderful music with shouting and laughter.

XIII

The Mayor was dumb, and the Council stood
As if they were changed into blocks of wood.
Unable to move a step, or cry
To the children merrily skipping by,
—Could only follow with the eye
That joyous crowd at the Piper's back.
But now the Mayor was on the rack,

And the wretched Council's bosoms beat,
As the Piper turned from the High Street
To where the Weser rolled its waters
Right in the way of their sons and daughters!
However he turned from South to West,
And to Koppelberg Hill his steps addressed,
And after him the children pressed;
Great was the joy in every breast.
"He never can cross that mighty top!
He's forced to let the piping drop,
And we shall see our children stop!"
When, lo, as they reached the mountainside,
A wondrous portal opened wide,
As if a cavern was suddenly hollowed;
And the Piper advanced and the children followed,
And when all were in to the very last,
The door in the mountainside shut fast.
Did I say, all? No! One was lame,
    And could not dance the whole of the way;
And in after years, if you would blame
    His sadness, he was used to say—
"It's dull in our town since my playmates left!
I can't forget that I'm bereft
Of all the pleasant sights they see,
Which the Piper also promised me.
For he led us, he said, to a joyous land,
Joining the town and just at hand,
Where waters gushed and fruit trees grew
And flowers put forth a fairer hue,
And everything was strange and new;
The sparrows were brighter than peacocks here,
And their dogs outran our fallow deer,
And honeybees had lost their stings,
And horses were born with eagles' wings:
And just as I became assured

My lame foot would be speedily cured,
The music stopped and I stood still,
And found myself outside the hill,
Left alone against my will,
To go now limping as before,
And never hear of that country more!"

XIV

Alas, alas for Hamelin!
    There came into many a burgher's pate
    A text which says that heaven's gate
    Opes to the rich at as easy rate
As the needle's eye takes a camel in!
The Mayor sent East, West, North, and South,
To offer the Piper, by word of mouth,
    Wherever it was men's lot to find him,
Silver and gold to his heart's content,
If he'd only return the way he went,
    And bring the children behind him.
And when they saw 'twas a lost endeavor,
And Piper and dancers were gone forever,
They made a decree that lawyers never
    Should think their records dated duly
If, after the day of the month and year,
These words did not as well appear,
"And so long after what happened here
    On the Twenty-second of July,
Thirteen hundred and seventy-six":
And the better in memory to fix
The place of the children's last retreat,
They called it, the Pied Piper's Street—
Where anyone playing on pipe or tabor
Was sure for the future to lose his labor.
Nor suffered they hostelry or tavern
    To shock with mirth a street so solemn;

But opposite the place of the cavern
    They wrote the story on a column,
And on the great church window painted
The same, to make the world acquainted
How their children were stolen away,
And there it stands to this very day.
And I must not omit to say
That in Transylvania there's a tribe
Of alien people who ascribe
The outlandish ways and dress
On which their neighbors lay such stress,
To their fathers and mothers having risen
Out of some subterraneous prison
Into which they were trepanned
Long time ago in a mighty band
Out of Hamelin town in Brunswick land,
But how or why, they don't understand.

              XV

So, Willy, let me and you be wipers
Of scores out with all men—especially pipers!
And, whether they pipe us free from rats or from mice,
If we've promised them aught, let us keep our promise!

ROBERT BROWNING

ELDORADO

Gaily bedight,
A gallant knight,
In sunshine and in shadow,
Had journeyed long,
Singing a song,
In search of Eldorado.

But he grew old—
This knight so bold—
And o'er his heart a shadow
Fell as he found
No spot of ground
That looked like Eldorado.

And, as his strength
Failed him at length,
He met a pilgrim shadow—
"Shadow," said he,
"Where can it be—
This land of Eldorado?"

"Over the Mountains
Of the Moon,
Down in the Valley of the Shadow,
Ride, boldly ride,"
The shade replied,
"If you seek for Eldorado."

EDGAR ALLAN POE

In the sixteenth century, Spanish explorers believed there was a city of fabulous riches in South America. Many of them searched for it, but the place existed only in their imaginations.

ANYONE LIVED IN
A PRETTY HOW TOWN

anyone lived in a pretty how town
(with up so floating many bells down)
spring summer autumn winter
he sang his didn't he danced his did.

Women and men(both little and small)
cared for anyone not at all
they sowed their isn't they reaped their same
sun moon stars rain

children guessed(but only a few
and down they forgot as up they grew
autumn winter spring summer)
that noone loved him more by more

when by now and tree by leaf
she laughed his joy she cried his grief
bird by snow and stir by still
anyone's any was all to her

someones married their everyones
laughed their cryings and did their dance
(sleep wake hope and then)they
said their nevers they slept their dream

stars rain sun moon
(and only the snow can begin to explain
how children are apt to forget to remember
with up so floating many bells down)

one day anyone died i guess
(and noone stooped to kiss his face)
busy folk buried them side by side
little by little and was by was

all by all and deep by deep
and more by more they dream their sleep
noone and anyone earth by april
wish by spirit and if by yes.

Women and men(both dong and ding)
summer autumn winter spring
reaped their sowing and went their came
sun moon stars rain

E. E. CUMMINGS

In addition to ignoring conventional rules of punctuation, E. E. Cummings also displaced words, often creating a puzzle for the reader to solve. This poem, for example, is the sweet story of two small people, anyone and noone, who find each other. And what does "a little how town" mean? It might be a small town where people are unaware that a wider world exists and simply ask "how?" What do you think?

A VISIT FROM ST. NICHOLAS

'Twas the night before Christmas, when all through the house
Not a creature was stirring, not even a mouse;
The stockings were hung by the chimney with care,
In hopes that St. Nicholas soon would be there;
The children were nestled all snug in their beds,
While visions of sugarplums danced in their heads;
And Mamma in her 'kerchief, and I in my cap,
Had just settled our brains for a long winter's nap—
When out on the lawn there arose such a clatter,
I sprang from my bed to see what was the matter.
Away to the window I flew like a flash,
Tore open the shutters, and threw up the sash.
The moon, on the breast of the new-fallen snow,
Gave the luster of midday to objects below;
When, what to my wondering eyes should appear,
But a miniature sleigh and eight tiny reindeer,
With a little old driver, so lively and quick,
I knew in a moment it must be St. Nick.
More rapid than eagles his coursers they came,
And he whistled, and shouted, and called them by name:
"Now, Dasher! now, Dancer! now, Prancer! and Vixen!
On, Comet! on, Cupid! on, Donder and Blitzen!
To the top of the porch! to the top of the wall!
Now dash away! dash away! dash away all!"
As dry leaves that before the wild hurricane fly,
When they meet with an obstacle, mount to the sky:
So up to the house-top the coursers they flew
With the sleigh full of toys, and St. Nicholas, too.

And then, in a twinkling, I heard on the roof
The prancing and pawing of each little hoof.
As I drew in my head, and was turning around,
Down the chimney St. Nicholas came with a bound.
He was dressed all in fur, from his head to his foot,
And his clothes were all tarnished with ashes and soot;
A bundle of toys he had flung on his back,
And he looked like a peddler just opening his pack.
His eyes—how they twinkled! his dimples, how merry!
His cheeks were like roses, his nose like a cherry!
His droll little mouth was drawn up like a bow,
And the beard on his chin was as white as the snow;
The stump of a pipe he held tight in his teeth,
And the smoke it encircled his head like a wreath;
He had a broad face, and a little round belly
That shook, when he laughed, like a bowl full of jelly.
He was chubby and plump, a right jolly old elf;
And I laughed when I saw him, in spite of myself.
A wink of his eye, and a twist of his head
Soon gave me to know I had nothing to dread.
He spoke not a word, but went straight to his work,
And he filled all the stockings; then turned with a jerk,
And laying his finger aside of his nose,
And giving a nod, up the chimney he rose.
He sprang to his sleigh, to his team gave a whistle,
And away they all flew like the down of a thistle.
But I heard him exclaim, ere he drove out of sight,
"Happy Christmas to all, and to all a good night!"

CLEMENT MOORE

Clement Moore, who was a professor of Greek and Oriental literature at a theological seminary in New York City, wanted to be known as a serious poet. Today he is remembered only for this poem, which he scribbled one winter evening to amuse his children.

THE HIGHWAYMAN

Many generations of schoolchildren had to memorize this popular poem. Alfred Noyes was best known as a poet, but he also wrote essays, plays, novels, and short stories. British and educated at Oxford, for nine years Noyes was a professor of English at Princeton University.

The wind was a torrent of darkness among the gusty trees,
The moon was a ghostly galleon tossed upon cloudy seas,
The road was a ribbon of moonlight over the purple moor,
And the highwayman came riding—
          Riding—riding—
The highwayman came riding, up to the old inn door.

He'd a French cocked hat on his forehead, a bunch of lace at
          his chin,
A coat of the claret velvet, and breeches of brown doeskin:
They fitted with never a wrinkle; his boots were up to the thigh!
And he rode with a jeweled twinkle,
          His pistol butts a-twinkle,
His rapier hilt a-twinkle, under the jeweled sky.

Over the cobbles he clattered and clashed in the dark inn yard,
And he tapped with his whip on the shutters, but all was locked
          and barred:
He whistled a tune to the window, and who should be waiting there
But the landlord's black-eyed daughter,
          Bess, the landlord's daughter,
Plaiting a dark red love-knot into her long black hair.

And dark in the dark old inn yard a stable wicket creaked
Where Tim, the ostler, listened; his face was white and peaked;
His eyes were hollows of madness, his hair like moldy hay,
But he loved the landlord's daughter,
          The landlord's red-lipped daughter;
Dumb as a dog he listened, and he heard the robber say—

"One kiss, my bonny sweetheart, I'm after a prize tonight,
But I shall be back with the yellow gold before the morning light;
Yet, if they press me sharply, and harry me through the day,
Then look for me by moonlight,
          Watch for me by moonlight:
I'll come to thee by moonlight, though hell should bar the way."

He rose upright in the stirrups; he scarce could reach her hand,
But she loosened her hair i' the casement! His face burned like
    a brand
As the black cascade of perfume came tumbling over his breast;
And he kissed its waves in the moonlight,
       (Oh, sweet black waves in the moonlight!)
Then he tugged at his rein in the moonlight, and galloped away
    to the West.

PART TWO

He did not come in the dawning; he did not come at noon;
And out o' the tawny sunset, before the rise o' the moon,
When the road was a gipsy's ribbon, looping the purple moor,
A redcoat troop came marching—
      Marching—marching—
King George's men came marching, up to the old inn door.

They said no word to the landlord, they drank his ale instead,
But they gagged his daughter and bound her to the foot of her
    narrow bed;
Two of them knelt at her casement, with muskets at their side!
There was death at every window;
      And Hell at one dark window;
For Bess could see, through her casement, the road that he
    would ride.

They had tied her up to attention, with many a sniggering jest;
They had bound a musket beside her, with the barrel beneath
    her breast!
"Now keep good watch!" and they kissed her.
      She heard the dead man say—
Look for me by moonlight;
      Watch for me by moonlight;
I'll come to thee by moonlight, though Hell should bar the way!

She twisted her hands behind her; but all the knots held good!
She writhed her hands till her fingers were wet with sweat
    or blood!
They stretched and strained in the darkness, and the hours
    crawled by like years,
Till now, on the stroke of midnight,
       Cold, on the stroke of midnight,
The tip of one finger touched it! The trigger at least was hers!

The tip of one finger touched it; she strove no more for the rest!
Up, she stood up to attention, with the barrel beneath her breast,
She would not risk their hearing: she would not strive again;
For the road lay bare in the moonlight;
       Blank and bare in the moonlight;
And the blood of her veins in the moonlight throbbed to her
    love's refrain.

Tlot-tlot; tlot, tlot! Had they heard it? The horse hoofs ringing clear;
Tlot-tlot; tlot-tlot, in the distance? Were they deaf that they
    did not hear?
Down the ribbon of moonlight, over the brow of the hill,
The highwayman came riding,
       Riding, riding!
The redcoats looked to their priming! She stood up, straight
    and still!

Tlot-tlot, in the frosty silence! *Tlot-tlot,* in the echoing night!
Nearer he came and nearer! Her face was like a light!
Her eyes grew wide for a moment; she drew one last deep breath,
Then her finger moved in the moonlight,
       Her musket shattered the moonlight,
Shattered her breast in the moonlight and warned him—with
    her death.

He turned; he spurred to the westward; he did not know who stood
Bowed, with her head o'er the musket, drenched with her own
    red blood!
Not till the dawn he heard it, his face grew gray to hear
How Bess, the landlord's daughter,
        The landlord's black-eyed daughter,
Had watched for her love in the moonlight, and died in the
    darkness there.

Back he spurred like a madman, shrieking a curse to the sky,
With the white road smoking behind him, and his rapier
    brandished high!
Blood-red were his spurs in the golden noon; wine-red was his
    velvet coat;
When they shot him down on the highway,
        Down like a dog on the highway,
And he lay in his blood on the highway, with a bunch of lace at
    his throat.

* * *

And still of a winter's night, they say, when the wind is in the trees,
When the moon is a ghostly galleon tossed upon cloudy seas,
When the road is a ribbon of moonlight over the purple moor,
A highwayman comes riding—
       Riding—riding—
A highwayman comes riding, up to the old inn door.

Over the cobbles he clatters and clangs in the dark inn yard;
And he taps with his whip on the shutters, but all is locked
    and barred;
He whistles a tune to the window, and who should be waiting there
       But the landlord's black-eyed daughter,
         Bess, the landlord's daughter,
Plaiting a dark red love-knot into her long black hair.

ALFRED NOYES

THE HOUSE WITH NOBODY IN IT

Whenever I walk to Suffern along the Erie track,
I go by a poor old farmhouse with its shingles broken
　　and black.
I suppose I've passed it a hundred times, but I always
　　stop for a minute,
And look at the house, the tragic house, the house
　　with nobody in it.

I never have seen a haunted house, but I hear there
　　are such things;
That they hold the talk of spirits, their mirth and
　　sorrowings.
I know this house isn't haunted, and I wish it were,
　　I do;
For it wouldn't be so lonely if it has a ghost or two.

This house on the road to Suffern needs a dozen
　　panes of glass,
And somebody out to weed the walk and take a scythe
　　to the grass.
It needs new paint and shingles, and the vines should be
　　trimmed and tied;
But what it needs the most of all is some people living
　　inside.

If I had a lot of money and all my debts were paid,
I'd put a gang of men to work with brush and saw
　　and spade.
I'd buy that place and fix it up the way it used to be
And I'd find some people who wanted a home and
　　give it to them free.

Now, a new house standing empty, with staring window
    and door,
Looks idle, perhaps, and foolish, like a hat on its block
    in the store.
But there's nothing mournful about it; it cannot be sad
    and lone
For the lack of something within it that it has never known.

But a house that has done what a house should do,
    a house that has sheltered life,
That has put its loving wooden arms around a man and
    his wife,
A house that has echoed a baby's laugh and held up his
    stumbling feet,
Is the saddest sight, when it's left alone, that ever your
    eyes could meet.

So whenever I go to Suffern along the Erie track,
I never go by the empty house without stopping and
    looking back,
Yet it hurts me to look at the crumbling roof and the
    shutters fallen apart,
For I can't help think the poor old house is a house with
    a broken heart.

JOYCE KILMER

THE WRECK OF THE HESPERUS

It was the schooner Hesperus,
    That sailed the wintry sea;
And the skipper had taken his little daughter,
    To bear him company.

Blue were her eyes as the fairy flax,
    Her cheeks like the dawn of day,
And her bosom white as the hawthorn buds,
    That ope in the month of May.

The skipper he stood beside the helm,
    His pipe was in his mouth,
And he watched how the veering flaw did blow
    The smoke now West, now South.

Then up and spake an old sailor,
    Had sailed to the Spanish Main,
"I pray thee, put into yonder port,
    For I fear a hurricane.

"Last night, the moon had a golden ring,
    And tonight no moon we see!"
The skipper, he blew a whiff from his pipe,
    And a scornful laugh laughed he.

Colder and louder blew the wind,
    A gale from the Northeast,
The snow fell hissing in the brine,
    And the billows frothed like yeast.

Down came the storm, and smote amain
    The vessel in its strength;
She shuddered and paused, like a frightened steed,
    Then leaped her cable's length.

"Come hither! come hither! my little daughter,
    And do not tremble so;
For I can weather the roughest gale
    That ever wind did blow."

He wrapped her warm in his seaman's coat
    Against the stinging blast;
He cut a rope from a broken spar,
    And bound her to the mast.

"O Father! I hear the church bells ring,
    Oh say, what may it be?"
" 'Tis a fog-bell on a rockbound coast!"
    And he steered for the open sea.

"O Father! I hear the sound of guns,
    Oh say, what may it be?"
"Some ship in distress, that cannot live
    In such an angry sea!"

"O Father! I see a gleaming light,
    Oh say, what may it be?"
But the father answered never a word,
    A frozen corpse was he.

Lashed to the helm, all stiff and stark,
    With his face turned to the skies,
The lantern gleamed through the gleaming snow
    On his fixed and glassy eyes.

Then the maiden clasped her hands and prayed
    That savèd she might be;
And she thought of Christ, who stilled the wave,
    On the Lake of Galilee.

And fast through the midnight dark and drear,
    Through the whistling sleet and snow,
Like a sheered ghost, the vessel swept
    Towards the reef of Norman's Woe.

In 1839, a ship was wrecked on a reef in Norman's Woe, near Gloucester in Massachusetts. Twenty bodies were washed ashore, including that of a woman lashed to a mast. It was on this actual shipwreck that Henry Wadsworth Longfellow based "The Wreck of the Hesperus," which was published the following year.

And ever the fitful gusts between
    A sound came from the land;
It was the sound of the trampling surf
    On the rocks and the hard sea-sand.

The breakers were right beneath her bows,
    She drifted a dreary wreck,
And a whooping billow swept the crew
    Like icicles from her deck.

She struck where the white and fleecy waves
    Looked soft as carded wool,
But the cruel rocks, they gored her side
    Like the horns of an angry bull.

Her rattling shrouds, all sheathed in ice,
    With the masts, went by the board;
Like a vessel of glass, she stove and sank,
    Ho! ho! the breakers roared!

At daybreak, on the bleak sea beach,
    A fisherman stood aghast,
To see the form of a maiden fair,
    Lashed close to a drifting mast.

The salt sea was frozen on her breast,
    The salt tears in her eyes;
And he saw her hair, like the brown seaweed,
    On the billow fall and rise.

Such was the wreck of the Hesperus,
    In the midnight and the snow!
Christ save us all from a death like this,
    On the reef of Norman's Woe!

HENRY WADSWORTH LONGFELLOW

THE VILLAGE BLACKSMITH

Under a spreading chestnut tree
    The village smithy stands;
The smith, a mighty man is he,
    With large and sinewy hands;
And the muscles of his brawny arms
    Are strong as iron bands.

His hair is crisp, and black, and long,
    His face is like the tan;
His brow is wet with honest sweat,
    He earns whate'er he can,
And looks the whole world in the face,
    For he owes not any man.

Week in, week out, from morn till night,
    You can hear his bellows blow;
You can hear him swing his heavy sledge,
    With measured beat and slow,
Like a sexton ringing the village bell,
    When the evening sun is low.

And children coming home from school
    Look in at the open door;
They love to see the flaming forge,
    And hear the bellows roar,
And catch the burning sparks that fly
    Like chaff from a threshing floor.

He goes on Sunday to the church,
    And sits among his boys;
He hears the parson pray and preach,
    He hears his daughter's voice,
Singing in the village choir,
    And it makes his heart rejoice.

Henry Wadsworth
Longfellow wrote this poem
about a blacksmith who
worked under a huge chestnut tree on Brattle Street in
Cambridge, Massachusetts,
near Longellow's home.
The tree was considered
dangerous to farmers who
drove under it and, despite
protests by many people,
including Longfellow, it was
cut down. Pieces of the tree
were saved, however, and
the children of Cambridge
collected money and had a
chair made from that wood.
They presented the chair
to Longfellow on his
seventy-second birthday.

It sounds to him like her mother's voice,
    Singing in Paradise.
He needs must think of her once more,
    How in the grave she lies;
And with his hard, rough hand he wipes
    A tear out of his eyes.

Toiling, rejoicing, sorrowing,
    Onward through life he goes;
Each morning sees some task begun,
    Each evening sees it close;
Something attempted, something done,
    Has earned a night's repose.

Thanks, thanks to thee, my worthy friend,
    For the lesson thou has taught!
Thus at the flaming forge of life
    Our fortunes must be wrought;
Thus on its sounding anvil shaped
    Each burning deed is thought!

HENRY WADSWORTH LONGFELLOW

LET'S PRETEND

∾ Fairies and witches, goblins and elves, giants and ogres, and even a charming little ghost are among the wonderful characters you'll meet in this enchanted land of Let's Pretend.

THE FAIRIES

There are fairies at the bottom of our garden!
        It's not so very, very far away;
You pass the gardener's shed and you just keep straight ahead—
        I do so hope they've really come to stay.
There's a little wood, with moss in it and beetles,
        And a little stream that quietly runs through;
You wouldn't think they'd dare to come merry-making there—
            Well, they do.

There are fairies at the bottom of our garden!
        They often have a dance on summer nights;
The butterflies and bees make a lovely little breeze,
        And the rabbits stand about and hold the lights.
Did you know that they could sit upon the moonbeams
        And pick a little star to make a fan,
And dance away up there in the middle of the air?
            Well, they can.

There are fairies at the bottom of our garden!
        You cannot think how beautiful they are;
They all stand up and sing when the Fairy Queen and King
        Come gently floating down upon their car.
The King is very proud and very handsome;
        The Queen—now can you guess who that could be
(She's a little girl all day, but at night she steals away)?
            Well—it's me!

ROSE FYLEMAN

I'D LOVE TO BE A FAIRY'S CHILD

Children born of fairy stock
Never need for shirt or frock,
Never want for food or fire,
Always get their heart's desire:
Jingle pockets full of gold,
Marry when they're seven years old.
Every fairy child may keep
Two strong ponies and ten sheep;
All have houses, each his own,
Built of brick or granite stone;
They live on cherries, they run wild—
I'd love to be a fairy's child.

ROBERT GRAVES

Robert Graves was born in London and attended the prestigious Charterhouse school. He joined the army to fight in World War I and then went to Oxford University. His first poems were published while he was still in the army. Although he considered himself primarily a poet, over the years he also wrote essays, novels, his autobiography, and works for children.

IN FAIRYLAND

The fairy poet takes a sheet
    Of moonbeam, silver white;
His ink is dew from daisies sweet,
    His pen a point of light.

My love I know is fairer far
    Than his, (though she is fair,)
And we should dwell where fairies are—
    For I could praise her there.

JOYCE KILMER

CATCHING FAIRIES

They're sleeping beneath the roses;
    Oh! kiss them before they rise,
And tickle their tiny noses,
    And sprinkle the dew on their eyes.
        Make haste, make haste;
        The fairies are caught;
          Make haste.

We'll put them in silver cages,
    And send them full-dress'd to court,
And maids of honor and pages
    Shall turn the poor things to sport.
        Be quick, be quick;
        Be quicker than thought;
          Be quick.

Their scarves shall be pennons for lancers,
    We'll tie up our flowers with their curls,
Their plumes will make fans for dancers,
    Their tears shall be set with pearls.
        Be wise, be wise;
        Make the most of the prize;
          Be wise.

They'll scatter sweet scents by winking,
    With sparks from under their feet;
They'll save us the trouble of thinking,
    Their voices will sound so sweet.
        Oh stay, oh stay:
        They're up and away:
          Oh stay!

WILLIAM CORY

William Cory taught at Eton, the famous English public school. He wrote poetry for adults and children as well as a number of educational works.

THE FAIRIES

Up the airy mountain,
 Down the rushy glen,
We daren't go a-hunting
 For fear of little men;
Wee folk, good folk,
 Trooping all together,
Green jacket, red cap,
 And white owl's feather!

Down along the rocky shore
 Some made their home,
They live on crispy pancakes
 Of yellow tide-foam;
Some in the reeds
 Of the black mountain lake,
With frogs for their watch dogs,
 All night awake.

High on the hill top
 The old King sits;
He is now so old and gray
 He's nigh lost his wits.
With a bridge of white mist
 Columbkill he crosses
On his stately journeys
 From Slieveleague to Rosses;

Or going up with music
 On cold starry nights,
To sup with the Queen
 Of the gay Northern Lights.

They stole little Bridget
    For seven years long;
When she came down again
    Her friends were all gone.
They took her lightly back,
    Between the night and morrow,
They thought that she was fast asleep,
    But she was dead with sorrow.
They have kept her ever since
    Deep within the lake,
On a bed of flag leaves,
    Watching till she wake.

By the craggy hillside,
    Through the mosses bare,
They have planted thorn trees
    For pleasure, here and there.
Is any man so daring
    As dig them up in spite,
He shall find their sharpest thorns
    In his bed at night.

Up the airy mountain,
    Down the rushy glen,
We daren't go a-hunting
    For fear of little men;
Wee folk, good folk,
    Trooping all together;
Green jacket, red cap,
    And white owl's feather!

WILLIAM ALLINGHAM

William Allingham was born in County Donegal in Ireland. He worked as a customs officer there and later in England. His first volume of poems was published when he was twenty-six years old and included this poem, "The Fairies," which is his best-known work.

THE PLUMPUPPETS

When little heads weary have gone to their bed,
When all the good nights and the prayers have been said,
Of all the good fairies that send bairns to rest
The little Plumpuppets are those I love best.

If your pillow is lumpy, or hot, thin, and flat,
The little Plumpuppets know just what they're at:
They plump up the pillow, all soft, cool, and fat—
    The little Plumpuppets plump-up it!

The little Plumpuppets are fairies of beds;
They have nothing to do but to watch sleepyheads;
They turn down the sheets and they tuck you in tight,
And they dance on your pillow to wish you good night!

CHRISTOPHER MORLEY

DREAMS

Beyond, beyond the mountain line,
    The gray stone and the boulder,
Beyond the growth of dark green pine,
    That crowns its western shoulder,
There lies that fairy land of mine,
    Unseen of a beholder.

Its fruits are all like rubies rare,
    Its streams are clear as glasses:
There golden castles hang in air,
    And purple grapes in masses,
And noble knights and ladies fair
    Come riding down the passes.

Ah me! they say if I could stand
    Upon those mountain ledges,
I should but see on either hand
    Plain fields and dusty hedges:
And yet I know my fairy land
    Lies somewhere o'er their hedges.

CECIL FRANCES ALEXANDER

THE BUTTERFLY'S BALL

"Come, take up your hats, and away let us haste
To the Butterfly's Ball and the Grasshopper's Feast;
The trumpeter, Gadfly, has summoned the crew,
And the revels are now only waiting for you."

So said little Robert, and pacing along,
His merry companions came forth in a throng,
And on the smooth grass by the side of a wood,
Beneath a broad oak that for ages had stood,
Saw the children of earth and the tenants of air
For an evening's amusement together repair.

And there came the Beetle, so blind and so black,
Who carried the Emmet, his friend, on his back;
And there was the Gnat and the Dragonfly, too,
With all their relations, green, orange, and blue.

And there came the Moth, with his plumage of down,
And the Hornet, in jacket of yellow and brown,
Who with him the Wasp, his companion, did bring:
They promised that evening to lay by their sting.

And the sly little Dormouse crept out of his hold,
And brought to the feast his blind brother, the Mole.
And the Snail, with his horns peeping out of his shell,
Came from a great distance—the length of an ell.

A mushroom their table, and on it was laid
A water-dock leaf, which a tablecloth made.
The viands were various, to each of their taste,
And the Bee brought her honey to crown the repast.

William Roscoe, an Englishman, was a banker, writer, scholar, and book collector, in addition to being a poet. He published this amusing poem, "The Butterfly's Ball," in 1806 and it has become a children's classic.

Then close on his haunches, so solemn and wise,
The Frog from a corner looked up to the skies;
And the Squirrel, well-pleased such diversions to see,
Mounted high overhead and looked down from a tree.

Then out came a Spider, with fingers so fine,
To show his dexterity on the tight line.
From one branch to another his cobwebs he slung,
Then quick as an arrow he darted along.

But just in the middle—oh! shocking to tell,
From his rope, in an instant, poor Harlequin fell.
Yet he touched not the ground, but with talons outspread,
Hung suspended in air, at the end of a thread.

Then the Grasshopper came, with a jerk and a spring,
Very long was his leg, though but short was his wing;
He took but three leaps, and was soon out of sight,
Then chirped his own praises the rest of the night.

With step so majestic, the Snail did advance,
And promised the gazers a minuet to dance:
But they all laughed so loud that he pulled in his head,
And went to his own little chamber to bed.
Then as evening gave way to the shadows of night,
Their watchman, the Glow-worm, came out with a light.

"Then home let us hasten while yet we can see,
For no watchman is waiting for you and for me."
So said little Robert, and pacing along,
His merry companions returned in a throng.

WILLIAM ROSCOE

THE CASTLE IN THE FIRE

The andirons were the dragons,
Set out to guard the gate
Of the old enchanted castle,
In the fire upon the grate.

We saw a turret window
Open a little space,
And frame, for just a moment,
A lady's lovely face:

Then, while we watched in wonder
From out the smoky veil,
A gallant knight came riding,
Dressed in coat of mail;

With slender lance a-tilting,
Thrusting with a skillful might,
He charged the crouching dragons—
Ah, 'twas a brilliant fight!

Then, in the roar and tumult,
The back log crashed in two,
And castle, knight, and dragons
Were hidden from our view;

But, when the smoke had lifted,
We saw, to our delight,
Riding away together,
The lady and the knight.

MARY JANE CARR

WHO KNOWS IF THE
MOON'S A BALLOON

who knows if the moon's
a balloon,coming out of a keen city
in the sky—filled with pretty people?
(and if you and i should

get into it,if they
should take me and take you into their balloon,
why then
we'd go up higher with all the pretty people

than houses and steeples and clouds:
go sailing
away and away sailing into a keen
city which nobody's ever visited, where

always
    it's
        Spring)and everyone's
in love and flowers pick themselves

E. E. CUMMINGS

THE UNSEEN PLAYMATE

When children are playing alone on the green
In comes the playmate that never was seen.
When children are happy and lonely and good,
The Friend of the Children comes out of the wood.

Nobody heard him and nobody saw,
His is a picture you never could draw,
But he's sure to be present, abroad or at home,
When children are happy and playing alone.

He lives in the laurels, he runs on the grass,
He sings when you tinkle the musical glass;
Whene'er you are happy and cannot tell why,
The Friend of the Children is sure to be by!

He loves to be little, he hates to be big,
'Tis he that inhabits the caves that you dig;
'Tis he when you play with your soldiers of tin
That sides with the Frenchmen and never can win.

'Tis he, when at night you go off to your bed,
Bids you go to your sleep and not trouble your head,
For wherever they're lying, in cupboard or shelf,
'Tis he will take care of your playthings himself!

ROBERT LOUIS STEVENSON

GOBLIN FEET

I am off down the road
Where the fairy lanterns glowed
And the little pretty flitter-mice are flying:
A slender band of gray
It runs creepily away
And the hedges and the grasses are a-sighing.
The air is full of wings,
And of blundery beetle-things
That warn you with their whirring and their humming.
O! I hear the tiny horns
Of enchanted leprechauns
And the padded feet of many gnomes a-coming!

O! the lights! O! the gleams! O! the little tinkly sounds!
O! the rustle of their noiseless little robes!
O! the echo of their feet—of their happy little feet!
O! their swinging lamps in little starlit globes.

I must follow in their train
Down the crooked fairy lane
Where the coney-rabbits long ago have gone,
And where silvery they sing
In a moving moonlit ring
All a-twinkle with the jewels they have on.
They are fading round the turn
Where the glow-worms palely burn
And the echo of their padding feet is dying!
O! it's knocking at my heart—
Let me go! O! let me start!
For the little magic hours are all a-flying.

O! the warmth! O! the hum! O! the colors in the dark!
O! the gauzy wings of golden honey-flies!
O! the music of their feet—of their dancing goblin feet!
O! the magic! O! the sorrow when it dies.

J. R. R. TOLKIEN

J.R.R. Tolkien was a professor of English language and literature at Oxford University. He published many academic works, but he is, perhaps, best-known for The Hobbit and its sequel The Lord of the Rings, which are based on his own mythology.

THE RIDE-BY-NIGHTS

Up on their brooms the Witches stream,
Crooked and black in the crescent's gleam,
One foot high, and one foot low,
Bearded, cloaked, and cowled, they go.
'Neath Charlie's Wane they twitter and tweet,
And away they swarm 'neath the Dragon's feet,
With a whoop and a flutter they swing and sway,
And surge pell-mell down the Milky Way.
Between the legs of the glittering Chair
They hover and squeak in the empty air.
Then round they swoop past the glimmering Lion
To where Sirius barks behind huge Orion;
Up, then, and over to wheel amain
Under the silver, and home again.

WALTER DE LA MARE

THE WITCHES' SONG

Thrice the brinded cat hath mew'd.
Thrice, and once the hedge pig whin'd.
Harper cries, " 'Tis time, 'tis time."
Round about the cauldron go;
In the poison'd entrails throw.
Toad, that under cold stone
Days and nights has thirty-one
Swelter'd venom sleeping got,
Boil thou first i' the charmed pot.
    Double, double toil and trouble;
    Fire burn and cauldron bubble.

Fillet of a fenny snake,
In the cauldron boil and bake;
Eye of newt, and toe of frog,
Wool of bat, and tongue of dog,
Adder's fork, and blind-worm's sting,
Lizard's leg, and howler's wing,
For a charm of powerful trouble,
Like a hell-broth boil and bubble.
    Double, double toil and trouble;
    Fire burn and cauldron bubble.

WILLIAM SHAKESPEARE

This most famous of witches' spells is from Act IV of William Shakespeare's play Macbeth.

THE WITCH OF WILLOWBY WOOD

There once was a witch of Willowby Wood,
and a weird wild witch was she, with hair that was snarled
and hands that were gnarled, and a kickety, rickety
knee. She could jump, they say,
to the moon and back, but this I never did see.
Now Willowby Wood was near Sassafras Swamp,
where there's never a road or rut. And there by the
singing witch-hazel bush the old woman builded
her hut. She builded with neither a hammer or shovel. She
kneaded, she rolled out, she baked
her brown hovel. For all witches' houses, I've oft heard
it said, are made of stick candy and fresh
gingerbread. But the shingles that shingled this old
witch's roof were lollipop shingles and hurricane-proof,
  too
hard to be pelted and melted by rain.
(Why this is important, I soon will explain.)
One day there came running to Sassafras Swamp a dark little
shadowy mouse. He was noted for being a scoundrel
and scamp. And he gnawed at the old woman's house
  where the
doorpost was weak and the doorpost was worn.
And when the witch scolded, he laughed her to scorn.
And when the witch chased him, he felt quite delighted.
  She
never could catch him for she was nearsighted. And so,
though she quibbled, he gnawed and he nibbled.
The witch said, "I won't have my house
take a tumble. I'll search in my magical book for a spell
I can weave and a charm I can mumble to get you
away from this nook. It will be a good warning to other
bad mice, who won't earn their bread
but go stealing a slice."

"Your charms cannot hurt," said the mouse, looking pert.
Well, she looked in her book and she
waved her right arm, and she said the most magical
things. Till the mouse, feeling strange,
looked about in alarm, and found he was growing some
wings. He flapped and he fluttered the longer she
  muttered.

"And now, my fine fellow,
you'd best be aloof," said the witch as he floundered
around. "You can't stay on earth and you
can't gnaw my roof. It's lollipop-hard and it's
hurricane-proof. So you'd better take off
from the ground. If you are wise, stay in the skies."
Then in went the woman of Willowby Wood,
in to her hearthstone and cat.
There she put her old volume up high on the shelf, and
fanned her hot face with her hat. Then she said,
"That is that! I have just made a *bat!*"

ROWENA BENNETT

THE SLEEPY GIANT

My age is three hundred and seventy-two,
 And I think, with the deepest regret,
How I used to pick up and voraciously chew
 The dear little boys whom I met.

I've eaten them raw, in their holiday suits;
 I've eaten them curried with rice;
I've eaten them baked, in their jackets and boots,
 And found them exceedingly nice.

But now that my jaws are too weak for such fare,
 I think it exceeding rude
To do such a thing, when I'm quite well aware
 Little boys do not like to be chewed.

And so I contentedly live upon eels,
 And try to do nothing amiss,
And I pass all the time I can spare from my meals
 In innocent slumber—like this.

CHARLES E. CARRYL

SONG OF THE OGRES

Little fellow, you're amusing,
Stop before you end up losing
    Your shirt:
Run along to Mother, Gus,
Those who interfere with us
    Get hurt.

Honest Virtue, old wives prattle,
Always wins the final battle,
    Dear, Dear!
Life's exactly what it looks,
Love may triumph in the books,
    Not here.

We're not joking, we assure you:
Those who rode this way before you
    Died hard.
What? Still spoiling for a fight?
Well, you asked for it all right:
    On guard!

Always hopeful, aren't you? Don't be.
Night is falling and it won't be
    Long now:
You will never see the dawn,
You will wish you'd not been born,
    And how!

W. H. AUDEN

W. H. Auden was born in York, England. He came to the United States when he was thirty-two years old, served in the American army as a major during World War II, and became an American citizen. One of the great poets of the twentieth century, he had a great range of styles and poetic forms.

THE DORCHESTER GIANT

There was a giant in times of old,
    A mighty one was he;
He had a wife, but she was a scold,
So he kept her shut in his mammoth fold;
    And he had children three.

It happened to be an election day,
    And the giants were choosing a king;
The people were not democrats then,
They did not talk of the rights of men,
    And all that sort of thing.

Then the giant took his children three,
    And fastened them in the pen;
The children roared; quoth the giant, "Be still!"
And Dorchester Heights and Milton Hill
    Rolled back the sound again.

Then he brought them a pudding stuffed with plums,
    As big as the State House dome;
Quoth he, "There's something for you to eat;
So stop your mouths with your 'lection treat,
    And wait till your dad comes home."

So the giant pulled him a chestnut stout,
    And whittled the boughs away;
The boys and their mother set up a shout,
Said he, "You're in and you can't get out,
    Bellow as loud as you may."

Off he went, and he growled a tune
    As he strode the fields along;
'Tis said a buffalo fainted away,
And fell as cold as a lump of clay,
    When he heard the giant's song.

But whether the story's true or not,
    It isn't for me to show;
There's many a thing that's twice as queer
In somebody's lectures that we hear,
    And those are true you know.

What are those lone ones doing now,
    The wife and the children sad?
Oh, they are in a terrible rout,
Screaming, and throwing their pudding about,
    Acting as they were mad.

They flung it over to Roxbury hills,
    They flung it over the plain,
And all over Milton and Dorchester, too
Great lumps of pudding the giants threw;
    They tumbled as thick as rain.

Giant and mammoth have passed away,
    For ages have floated by;
The suet is hard as a marrowbone,
And every plum is turned to a stone,
    But there the puddings lie.

And if, some pleasant afternoon,
    You'll ask me out to ride,
The whole of the story I will tell,
And you shall see where the puddings fell,
    And pay for the punch beside.

OLIVER WENDELL HOLMES

Oliver Wendell Holmes was born in Boston. He was a distinguished doctor as well as a world-renowned writer of poetry, essays, novels, and books on medical subjects. He got his medical degree at Harvard and for many years taught there. This amusing poem about a mighty giant is set in the Boston area, as anyone who lives there will realize.

OUR LITTLE GHOST

Oft, in the silence of the night,
    When the lonely moon rides high,
When wintry winds are whistling,
    And we hear the owl's shrill cry,
In the quiet, dusky chamber,
    By the flickering firelight,
Rising up between two sleepers,
    Comes a spirit all in white.

A winsome little ghost it is,
    Rosy-cheeked, and bright of eye;
With yellow curls all breaking loose
    From the small cap pushed awry.
Up it climbs among the pillows,
    For the "big dark" brings no dread
And a baby's boundless fancy
    Makes a kingdom of a bed.

A fearless little ghost it is;
    Safe the night seems as the day;
The moon is but a gentle face,
    And the sighing winds are gay.
The solitude is full of friends,
    And the hour brings no regrets;
For in this happy little soul,
    Shines a sun that never sets.

A merry little ghost it is,
    Dancing gaily by itself,
On the flowery counterpane,
    Like a tricksy household elf;
Nodding to the fitful shadows,
    As they flicker on the wall;
Talking to familiar pictures,
    Mimicking the owl's shrill call.

A thoughtful little ghost it is;
    And, when lonely gambols tire,
With chubby hands on chubby knees,
    It sits winking at the fire.
Fancies innocent and lovely
    Shine before those baby eyes—
Endless fields of dandelions,
    Brooks, and birds, and butterflies.

A loving little ghost it is:
    When crept into its nest,
Its hand on Father's shoulder laid,
    Its head on Mother's breast,
It watches each familiar face,
    With a tranquil, trusting eye;
And, like a sleepy little bird,
    Sings its own soft lullaby.

Then those who feigned to sleep before,
    Lest baby play till dawn,
Wake and watch their folded flower—
    Little rose without a thorn.
And, in the silence of the night,
    The hearts that love it most
Pray tenderly above its sleep,
    "God bless our little ghost!"

LOUISA MAY ALCOTT

Louisa May Alcott, who was born in Pennsylvania, is best known for her novels, the most famous of which is Little Women. *But she was also the editor of a children's magazine, wrote a book called* Hospital Sketches *about her experiences as a nurse during the Civil War, and poems like this one about a much-loved baby ghost.*

John Kendrick Banks, who was born in Yonkers, New York, was an editor of Life *and* Harper's Magazine. *He wrote more than thirty volumes of humor and verse, and his poems and sketches were frequently published in children's magazines.*

THE LITTLE ELF

I met a little elf-man once,
Down where the lilies blow.
I asked him why he was so small
And why he didn't grow.

He slightly frowned, and with his eye
He looked me through and through.
"I'm quite as big for me," said he,
"As you are big for you."

JOHN KENDRICK BANGS

SPECIAL PLACES

In this section, such well known poets as William Butler Yeats, Dylan Thomas, and William Wordsworth write of places that were special to them. Also included are Samuel Coleridge's famous poem, "Kubla Khan," about a place he visited only in a dream, and Countee Cullen's poem about Africa, the special place of his heritage.

FERN HILL

Dylan Thomas was born in Glamorganshire, Wales, the son of a school-teacher. He was an accomplished poet while he was still in his teens and his first book of poems was published before he was twenty-one. He had a marvelous voice and he read his poetry aloud in person and on records. Fern Hill was the name of his aunt's country house, where he spent time as a boy. This is considered one of his finest poems.

Now as I was young and easy under the apple boughs
About the lilting house and happy as the grass was green,
    The night above the dingle starry,
        Time let me hail and climb
    Golden in the heydays of his eyes,
And honored among wagons I was prince of the apple towns
And once below a time I lordly had the trees and leaves
        Trail with daisies and barley
    Down the rivers of the windfall light.

And as I was green and carefree, famous among the barns
About the happy yard and singing as the farm was home,
    In the sun that is young once only,
        Time let me play and be
    Golden in the mercy of his means,
And green and golden I was huntsman and herdsman, the calves
Sang in my horn, the foxes on the hills barked clear and cold,
        And the sabbath rang slowly
    In the pebbles of the holy streams.

All the sun long it was running, it was lovely, the hay
Fields high as the house, the tunes from the chimneys, it was air
    And playing, lovely and watery
        And fire green as grass.
    And nightly under the simple stars
As I rode to sleep the owls were bearing the farm away,
All the moon long I heard, blessed among stables, the nightjars
    Flying with the ricks, and the horses
        Flashing into the dark.

And then to awake, and the farm, like a wanderer white
With the dew, come back, the cock on his shoulder: it was all
     Shining, it was Adam and maiden,
          The sky gathered again
     And the sun grew round that very day.
So it must have been after the birth of the simple light
In the first, spinning place, the spellbound horses walking warm
     Out of the whinnying green stable
          On to the fields of praise.

And honored among foxes and pheasants by the gay house
Under the new made clouds and happy as the heart was long,
     In the sun born over and over,
          I ran my heedless ways,
     My wishes raced through the house high hay
And nothing I cared, at my sky blue trades, that time allows
In all his tuneful turning so few and such morning songs
     Before the children green and golden
          Follow him out of grace,

Nothing I cared, in the lamb white days, that time would take me
Up to the swallow thronged loft by the shadow of my hand,
     In the moon that is always rising,
          Not that riding to sleep
     I should hear him fly with the high fields
And wake to the farm forever fled from the childless land.
Oh as I was young and easy in the mercy of his means,
          Time held me green and dying
     Though I sang in my chains like the sea.

DYLAN THOMAS

KUBLA KHAN

In Xanadu did Kubla Khan
A stately pleasure dome decree:
Where Alph, the sacred river, ran
Through caverns measureless to man
Down to a sunless sea.
So twice five miles of fertile ground
With walls and towers were girdled round:
And here were gardens bright with sinuous rills,
Where blossom'd many an incense-bearing tree;
And here were forests ancient as the hills,
Enfolding sunny spots of greenery.

But oh! that deep romantic chasm which slanted
Down the green hill athwart a cedarn cover!
A savage place! as holy and enchanted
As e'er beneath a waning moon was haunted
By a woman wailing for her demon lover!
And from this chasm, with ceaseless turmoil seething,
As if this earth in fast thick pants were breathing,
A mighty fountain momently was forced;
Amid whose swift half-intermittent burst
Huge fragments vaulted like rebounding hail,
Or chaffy grain beneath the thresher's flail:
And 'mid these dancing rocks at once and ever
It flung up momently the sacred river.
Five miles meandering with a mazy motion
Through wood and dale the sacred river ran,
Then reach'd the caverns measureless to man.
And sank in tumult to a lifeless ocean:
And 'mid this tumult Kubla heard from far
Ancestral voices prophesying war!

The shadow of the dome of pleasure
Floated midway on the waves;
Where was heard the mingled measure
From the fountain and the caves.
It was a miracle of rare device,
A sunny pleasure dome with caves of ice!

A damsel with a dulcimer
In a vision once I saw:
It was an Abyssinian maid,
And on her dulcimer she play'd,
Singing of Mount Abora.
Could I revive within me,
Her symphony and song,
To such a deep delight 'twould win me,
That with music loud and long,
I would build that dome in air,
That sunny dome! those caves of ice!
And all who hear should see them there,
And all should cry, Beware! Beware!
His flashing eyes, his floating hair!
Weave a circle round him thrice,
And close your eyes with holy dread,
For he on honey-dew hath fed,
And drunk the milk of Paradise.

SAMUEL TAYLOR COLERIDGE

Samuel Coleridge fell asleep in a chair one day and after three hours of vivid dreaming he awoke and wrote down the beginning of a much longer poem that had formed in his mind. Then he was called away on business and later, when he returned to his room, he could no longer remember his dream and all that remained is this poem about Kubla Khan and his pleasure dome in Xanadu.

COMPOSED UPON WESTMINSTER BRIDGE

Earth has not anything to show more fair:
Dull would he be of soul who could pass by
A sight so touching in its majesty:
This City now doth, like a garment, wear
The beauty of the morning: silent, bare,
Ships, towers, domes, theaters, and temples lie
Open unto the fields, and to the sky;
All bright and glittering in the smokeless air.
Never did sun more beautifully steep
In his first splendor, valley, rock, or hill;
Ne'er saw I, never felt, a calm so deep!
The river glideth as his own sweet will:
Dear God! the very houses seem asleep;
And all that mighty heart is lying still!

WILLIAM WORDSWORTH

Early on a sunny September morning, William Wordsworth and his sister, Dorothy, crossed the Thames in a coach on their way to France. The city looked so beautiful that Wordsworth was inspired to write this poem.

THE LAKE ISLE OF INNISFREE

I will arise and go now, and go to Innisfree,
And a small cabin build there, of clay and wattles made:
Nine bean-rows will I have there, a hive for the honey bee,
And live alone in the bee-loud glade.

And I shall have some peace there, for peach come dropping slow,
Dropping from the veils of the morning to where the cricket sings;
There midnight's all a-glimmer, and noon a purple glow,
And evening full of the linnet's wings.

I will arise and go now for always night and day
I hear lake water lapping with low sounds by the shore;
While I stand on the roadway, or on the pavements gray,
I hear it in the deep heart's core.

WILLIAM BUTLER YEATS

Innisfree is pro-nounced "Innishfree" and in Gallic, the language of Ireland, it means "Heather Island." That explains "noon a purple glow" which describes the reflection of heather in the water. Yeats explains that he was inspired to write this poem, one of his earliest, when he was walking down Fleet Street in London and became very homesick when he "heard a little trickle of water and a saw a fountain in a shop window. . . and began to remember lake water. "From the sudden remembrance," he wrote, "came my poem 'Innisfree,' my first lyric with anything in its rhythm of my own music."

OUT WHERE THE WEST BEGINS

In 1912, the governors of the Western states met in Buffalo, New York, and it was reported in the newpapers of the day that they argued about just where the West began. This gave Arthur Chapman, a journalist, the idea for this popular, and much recited, poem.

Out where the handclasp's a little stronger,
Out where the smile dwells a little longer,
    That's where the West begins;
Out where the sun is a little brighter,
Where the snows that fall are a trifle whiter,
Where the bonds of home are a wee bit tighter,
    That's where the West begins.

Out where the skies are a trifle bluer,
Out where friendship's a little truer,
    That's where the West begins;
Out where a fresher breeze is blowing;
Where there's laughter in every streamlet flowing,
Where there's more of reaping and less of sowing,
    That's where the West begins.

Out were the world is in the making,
Where fewer hearts in despair are aching,
    That's where the West begins;
Where there's more of singing and less of sighing,
Where there's more of giving and less of buying,
And a man makes friends without half trying—
    That's where the West begins.

ARTHUR CHAPMAN

HERITAGE

What is Africa to me:
Copper sun or scarlet sea,
Jungle star or jungle track,
Strong bronzed men, or regal black
Women from whose loins I sprang
When the birds of Eden sang?
One three centuries removed
From the scenes his father loved,
Spicy grove, cinnamon tree,
What is Africa to me?

COUNTEE CULLEN

Countee Cullen was born in New York City and was educated at New York University and Harvard. An African American poet of enormous talent, he became widely known after his first book was published when he was twenty-two. He taught junior high school in New York and, in addition to writing a novel and poetry, he wrote stories for children which have been collected in two books.

INDIAN NAMES

Ye say they all have passed away,
    That noble race and brave,
That their light canoes have vanished
    From off the crested wave;
That 'mid the forests where they roamed
    There rings no hunters' shout,
But their names is on your waters,
    Ye may not wash it out.

'Tis where Ontario's billow
    Like ocean's surge is curled,
Where strong Niagara's thunders wake
    The echo of the world,
Where red Missouri bringeth
    Rich tribute from the west,
And Rappahannock sweetly sleeps
    On green Virginia's breast.

Ye say their conelike cabins
    That clustered o'er the vale,
Have disappeared, as withered leaves
    Before the autumn's gale;
But their memory liveth on your hills,
    Their baptism on your shore,
Your everlasting rivers speak
    Their dialect of yore.

Old Massachusetts wears it,
    Within her lordly crown,
And broad Ohio bears it,
    Amid his young renown;
Connecticut hath wreathed it
    Where her quiet foliage waves,
And bold Kentucky breathes it hoarse
    Through all her ancient caves.

Wachuset hides its lingering voice
    Within his rocky heart,
And Allegheny graves its tone
    Throughout his lofty chart.
Monadnock on his forehead hoar
    Doth seal the sacred trust,
Your mountains build their monument,
    Though yet destroy their dust.

Ye call these red-browed brethren
    The insects of an hour,
Crushed like the noteless worm amid
    The regions of their power;
Ye drive them from their father's lands,
    Ye break of faith the seal,
But can ye from the court of Heaven
    Exclude their last appeal?

Ye see their unresisting tribes,
    With toilsome step and slow,
On through the trackless desert pass,
    A caravan of woe;
Think ye the Eternal's ear is deaf?
    His sleepless vision dim?
Think ye the soul's blood may not cry
    From that far land to him?

LYDIA HUNTLEY SIGOURNEY

"How can the red men be forgotten, while so many of our states and territories, bays, lakes, and rivers, are indelibly stamped by names of their giving?" wrote Lydia Huntley Sigourney more than one hundred years ago. She wrote this poem, naming many of these places, as a tribute to Native Americans.

ADLESTROP

Yes, I remember Adlestrop—
The name, because one afternoon
Of heat the express train drew up there
Unwontedly. It was late June.

The steam hissed. Someone cleared his throat.
No one left and no one came
On the bare platform. Where I was
Was Adlestrop—only the name
And willows, will-herb, and grass,
And meadowsweet, and haycocks dry,
No whit less still and lone fair
Than the high cloudlets in the sky.

And for the minute a blackbird sang
Close by, and round him, mistier,
Farther and farther, all the birds
Of Oxfordshire and Gloucestershire.

EDWARD THOMAS

✎ *Aldlestrop is a village in Gloucestershire, England. This poem was written more than one hundred years ago and neither the railroad nor the station still exist, but one of the station signs is preserved in a village garden.*

POEMS TO PONDER

～ The selections in this section are all poems that are good to think about. Two of them are about books, another is about music. There is John Milton's famous sonnet on his blindness, and two fine poems written by Robert Frost. Other writers whose poems are included are Maya Angelou, Rudyard Kipling, and Robert Wilbur. Read each of them slowly—and allow time to think and talk about it.

THERE IS NO FRIGATE
LIKE A BOOK

There is no frigate like a book
    To take us lands away,
Nor any coursers like a page
    Of prancing poetry.
This traverse may the poorest take
    without oppress of toll;
How frugal is the chariot
    That bears a human soul!

EMILY DICKINSON

BOOKS FALL OPEN

Books fall open,
you fall in,
delighted where
you've never been;
hear voices not once
heard before,
reach world on world
through door on door;
find unexpected
keys to things
locked up beyond
imaginings.
What might you be,
perhaps become,
because one book
is somewhere? Some
wise delver into
wisdom, wit,
and wherewithal
has written it,
True books will venture,
dare you out,
whisper secrets,
maybe shout
across the gloom
to you in need,
who hanker for
a book to read.

DAVID MCCORD

Amy Lowell was born in Brookline, Massachusetts, into a wealthy and prominent New England family. She was one of the first so called imagist poets in the United States, breaking with tradition and writing poems that did not rhyme and were about any subject the writer chose. She went on lecture and reading tours and with her enormous enthusiasm and theatrical presence she excited audiences and was successful in bringing American poetry into the twentieth century.

MUSIC

The neighbor sits in his window and plays the flute.
From my bed I can hear him,
And the round notes flutter and tap about the room,
And hit against each other,
Blurring to unexpected chords.
It is very beautiful,
With the little flute-notes all about me,
In the darkness.

In the daytime,
The neighbor eats bread and onions with one hand
And copies music with the other.
He is fat and has a bald head,
So I do not look at him,
But run quickly past his window.
There is always the sky to look at,
Or the water in the well!

But when night comes and he plays his flute,
I think of him as a young man,
With gold seals hanging from his watch,
And a blue coat with silver buttons.
As I lie in my bed
The flute-notes push against my ears and lips.
And I go to sleep, dreaming.

AMY LOWELL

The Bells

I

Hear the sledges with the bells—
Silver bells!
What a world of merriment their melody foretells!
How they tinkle, tinkle, tinkle,
In the icy air of night!
While the stars that oversprinkle
All the heavens, seem to twinkle
With a crystalline delight;
Keeping time, time, time,
In a sort of tunic rhyme,
To the tintinnabulation that so musically wells
From the bells, bells, bell, bells,
Bells, bells, bells—
From the jingling and the tinkling of the bells.

II

Hear the mellow wedding bells—
Golden bells!
What a world of happiness their harmony foretells!
Through the balmy air of night
How they ring out their delight!—
From the molten-golden notes,
And all in tune,
What a liquid ditty floats
To the turtledove that listens, while she gloats
On the moon!
Oh, from out the sounding cells,
What a gush of euphony voluminously wells!
How it swells!
How it dwells
On the Future!—how it tells
Of the rapture that impels

To the swinging and the ringing
Of the bells, bells, bells—
Of the bells, bells, bells, bells,
Bells, bells, bells—
To the rhyming and the chiming of the bells!

III
Hear the loud alarum bells—
Brazen bells!
What a tale of terror, now, their turbulency tells!
In the startled ear of night
How they scream out their affright!
Too much horrified to speak,
They can only shriek, shriek,
Out of tune,
In a clamorous appealing to the mercy of the fire,
In a mad expostulation with the deaf and frantic fire,
Leaping higher, higher, higher,
With a desperate desire,
And a resolute endeavor
Now—now to sit, or never,
By the side of the palefaced moon.
Oh, the bells, bells, bells!
What a tale their terror tells
Of Despair!
How they clang, and clash, and roar!
What a horror they outpour
On the bosom of the palpitating air!
Yet the ear, it fully knows,
By the twanging
And the clanging,
How the danger ebbs and flows;
Yet the ear distinctly tells,
In the jangling
And the wrangling,

How the danger sinks and swells,
By the sinking or the swelling in the anger of the bells—
Of the bells,—
Of the bells, bells, bells, bells,
Bells, bells, bells—
In the clamor and the clangor of the bells!

IV
Hear the tolling of the bells—
Iron bells!
What a world of solemn thought their monody compels!
In the silence of the night,
How we shiver with affright
At the melancholy menace of their tone!
For every sound that floats
From the rust within their throats
Is a groan.
And the people—ah, the people—
They that dwell up in the steeple,
All alone,
And who tolling, tolling, tolling,
In that muffled monotone,
Feel a glory in so rolling
On the human heart a stone—
They are neither man nor woman—
They are neither brute nor human—
They are Ghools:
And their king it is who tolls:
And he rolls, rolls, rolls,
Rolls
A paean from the bells!
And his merry bosom swells
With the paean of the bells!
And he dances, and he yells;
Keeping time, time, time,

In a sort of Runic rhyme,
To the paean of the bells—
Of the bells:
Keeping time, time, time,
In a sort of Runic rhyme,
To the throbbing of the bells—
Of the bells, bells, bells—
To the sobbing of the bells;
Keeping time, time, time,
As he knells, knells, knells,
In a happy Runic rhyme,
To the rolling of the bells—
Of the bells, bells, bells:—
To the tolling of the bells—
Of the bells, bells, bells, bells,
Bells, bells, bells—
To the moaning and the groaning of the bells.

EDGAR ALLAN POE

SOME OPPOSITES

The opposite of *standing still*
Is *walking up or down a hill*,
Running backwards, creeping, crawling,
Leaping off a cliff and falling,
Turning somersaults in gravel,
Or any other mode of travel.

The opposite of *doughnut?* Wait
A minute while I meditate.
This isn't easy. Ah, I've found it!
A cookie with a hole around it.

What is the opposite of *two?*
A lonely me, a lonely you.

The opposite of a *cloud* could be
A *white reflection in the sea*,
Or *a huge blueness in the air*,
Caused by a cloud's not being there.

The opposite of *opposite?*
That's much too difficult. I quit.

RICHARD WILBUR

*Richard Wilbur, his
wife, and their four children
used to play an unusual
game around the dinner
table. One member of the
family would suggest a word,
and then everyone would
join in a lively quarrel about
its proper opposite. In his
book* Opposites, *from which
these rhymes are taken, the
world-famous poet shares
his family's game.*

John Milton became blind when he was forty-three years old, but despite this he went on to compose many great poems until his death twenty-three years later, in 1674. He wrote this moving sonnet in 1652, when he had been blind for about a year, at the time that his great epic, Paradise Lost, was taking shape in his mind.

SONNET ON HIS BLINDNESS

When I consider how my light is spent
 Ere half my days, in this dark world and wide,
 And that one talent, which is death to hide,
 Lodged with me useless, though my soul more bent
To serve therewith my Maker, and present
 My true account, lest He, returning, chide:
 "Doth God exact day labor, light denied?"
 I fondly ask. But Patience, to prevent
That murmur, soon replies, "God doth not need
 Either man's work, or His own gifts; who best
 Bear His mild yoke, they serve Him best. His state
Is kingly. Thousands at His bidding speed,
 And post o'er land and ocean without rest;
 They also serve who only stand and wait."

JOHN MILTON

When I Have Fears
That I May Cease to Be

When I have fears that I may cease to be
    Before my pen has gleaned my teaming brain,
Before high-piled books, in charactery,
    Hold like rich garners the full ripened grain:
When I behold, upon the night's starred face,
    Huge cloudy symbols of a high romance,
And think that I may never live to trace
    Their shadows, with the magic hand of chance;
And when I feel, fair creature of an hour,
    That I shall never look upon thee more,
Never have relish in the faery power
    Of unreflecting love—then on the shore
Of the wide world I stand alone, and think
    Till love and fame to nothingness do sink.

JOHN KEATS

When John Keats wrote this sonnet he knew that he would soon die of tuberculosis. He did, indeed, die at the age of twenty-six leaving a body of work that assured his fame.

Born in Bombay, India, Rudyard Kipling was sent to school in England when he was six years old. He returned to India eleven years later and began his career as a journalist, novelist, and poet. Generations of children have been delighted by the stories in his Jungle books. "If—" is one of the most popular inspirational poems ever written. It is often seen framed in offices and schools and is frequently quoted on graduation cards.

IF—

If you can keep your head when all about you
    Are losing theirs and blaming it on you;
If you can trust yourself when all men doubt you,
    But make allowance for their doubting too;
If you can wait and not be tired by waiting,
    Or, being lied about, don't deal in lies,
Or, being hated, don't give way to hating,
    And yet don't look too good, nor talk too wise;

If you can dream—and not make dreams your master;
    If you can think—and not make thoughts your aim;
If you can meet with triumph and disaster
    And treat those two imposters just the same;
If you can bear to hear the truth you've spoken
    Twisted by knaves to make a trap for fools,
Or watch the things you gave your life to, broken,
    And stoop and build 'em up with worn-out tools;

If you can make one heap of all your winnings
    And risk it on one turn of pitch-and-toss,
And lose, and start again at your beginnings
    And never breathe a word about your loss;
If you can force your heart and nerve and sinew
    To serve your turn long after they are gone,
And so hold on when there is nothing in you
    Except the Will which says to them: "Hold on!"

If you can talk with crowds and keep your virtue,
    Or walk with kings—nor lose the common touch;
If neither foes nor loving friends can hurt you;
    If all men count with you, but none too much;
If you can fill the unforgiving minute
    With sixty seconds' worth of distance run—
Yours is the Earth and everything that's in it,
    And—which is more—you'll be a Man, my son!

RUDYARD KIPLING

HOPE

"Hope" is the thing with feathers
That perches in the soul,
And sings the tune without the words,
And never stops at all,

And sweetest in the gale is heard;
And sore must be the storm
That could abash the little bird
That keeps so many warm.

I've heard it in the chillest land,
And on the strangest sea;
Yet, never, in extremity,
It asked a crumb of me.

EMILY DICKINSON

ABOU BEN ADHEM

∿ *Leigh Hunt did not actually write this poem. It is his translation of a French poem based on an Islamic legend that tells how Allah, on the night of a particular feast day, checks in a golden book the names of those who love him.*

Abou Ben Adhem (may his tribe increase!)
Awoke one night from a deep dream of peace,
And saw, within the moonlight in his room,
Making it rich, and like a lily in bloom,
An angel writing in a book of gold:
Exceeding peace had made Ben Adhem bold,
And to the Presence in the room he said,
"What writest thou?" The vision raised its head,
And with a look made of all sweet accord
Answered, "The names of those who love the Lord."
"And is mine one?" said Abou. "Nay, not so,"
Replied the angel. Abou spoke more low,
But cheerily still; and said, "I pray thee, then,
Write me as one that loves his fellow men."

The angel wrote, and vanished. The next night
It came again with a great wakening light,
And showed the names whom love of God had blessed,
And, lo! Ben Adhem's name led all the rest.

LEIGH HUNT

PRECIOUS STONES

An emerald is as green as grass,
    A ruby red as blood,
A sapphire shines as blue as heaven,
    But a flint lies in the mud.

A diamond is a brilliant stone
    To catch the world's desire,
An opal holds a rainbow light,
    But a flint holds fire.

CHRISTINA ROSSETTI

WHAT IS PINK?

What is pink? A rose is pink
By the fountain's brink.
What is red? A poppy's red
In its barley bed.
What is blue? The sky is blue
Where the clouds float through.
What is white? A swan is white
Sailing in the light.
What is yellow? Pears are yellow,
Rich and ripe and mellow.
What is green? The grass is green,
With small flowers between.
What is violet? Clouds are violet
In the summer twilight.
What is orange? Why, an orange,
Just an orange!

CHRISTINA ROSSETTI

STOPPING BY WOODS ON A SNOWY EVENING

Whose woods these are I think I know.
His house is in the village though;
He will not see me stopping here
To watch his woods fill up with snow.

My little horse must think it queer
To stop without a farmhouse near
Between the woods and frozen lake
The darkest evening of the year.

He gives his harness bells a shake
To ask if there is some mistake.
The only other sound's the sweep
Of easy wind and downy flake.

The woods are lovely, dark, and deep.
But I have promises to keep,
And miles to go before I sleep,
And miles to go before I sleep.

ROBERT FROST

Born in San Francisco, Robert Frost settled permanently on a farm in New Hampshire after several jobs as a laborer and a period of farming in New England. He was never graduated from college, but he won twenty-five honorary degrees, and was the only poet to receive four Pulitzer Prizes. He said that he wrote this poem almost effortlessly one morning after staying up all night to work on a long poem. It was his favorite poem. He called it "my best bid for remembrance."

THE ROAD NOT TAKEN

Two roads diverged in a yellow wood,
And sorry I could not travel both
And by one traveler, long I stood
And looked down one as far as I could
To where it bent in the undergrowth;

Then took the other, as just as fair,
And having perhaps the better claim,
Because it was grassy and wanted wear;
Though as for that, the passing there
Had worn them really about the same,

And both that morning equally lay
In leaves no step had trodden black.
Oh, I kept the first for another day!
Yet knowing how way leads on to way,
I doubted if I should ever come back.

I shall be telling this with a sigh
Somewhere ages and ages hence:
Two roads diverged in a wood, and I—
I took the one less traveled by,
And that has made all the difference.

ROBERT FROST

THE WAY THROUGH THE WOODS

They shut the road through the woods
Seventy years ago.
Weather and rain have undone it again.
And now you would never know
There was once a path through the woods
Before they planted the trees.
It is underneath the coppice and heath
And the thin anemones.
Only the keeper sees
That, where the ring dove broods,
And the badgers roll at ease,
There was once a road through the woods.

Yet, if you enter the woods
Of a summer evening late,
When the air cools on the trout-ringed pools
Where the otter whistles his mate,
(They fear not men in the woods
Because they see so few.)
You will hear the beat of a horse's feet
And the swish of a skirt in the dew,
Steadily cantering through
The misty solitudes,
As though they perfectly knew
The old lost road through the woods . . .
But there is no road through the woods.

RUDYARD KIPLING

From PRELUDES

The winter evening settles down
With smells of steaks in passageways.
Six o'clock.
The burnt-out ends of smoky days
And now a gusty shower wraps
The grimy scraps
Of withered leaves about your feet
And newspapers from vacant lots;
The showers beat
On broken blinds and chimney pots,
And at the corner of the street
A lonely cab-horse steams and stamps.
And then the lighting of the lamps.

T. S. ELIOT

T.S. Eliot was born in St. Louis, Missouri, and went to Harvard University. When he was twenty-six years old he emigrated to England and eventually became a British subject. The imagery in this poem exemplifies his belief that "The essential advantage for a poet is not to have a beautiful world with which to deal; it is to be able to see beneath both beauty and ugliness; to see the boredom, and the horror, and the glory."

SEA FEVER

I must go down to the seas again, to the lonely sea and the sky,
And all I ask is a tall ship and a star to steer her by;
And the wheel's kick and the wind's song and the white sail's
    shaking,
And a gray mist on the sea's face, and a gray dawn breaking.

I must go down to the seas again, for the call of the running
    tide
Is a wild call and a clear call that may not be denied;
And all I ask is a windy day with the white clouds flying,
And the flung spray and the blown spume, and the sea gulls
    crying.

I must go down to the seas again, to the vagrant gypsy life,
To the gull's way and the whale's way where the wind's like
    a whetted knife;
And all I ask is a merry yarn from a laughing fellow-rover,
And quiet sleep and a sweet dream when the long trick's over.

JOHN MASEFIELD

SEA SHELL

Sea Shell, Sea Shell,
Sing me a song, O please!
A song of ships, and sailormen,
And parrots, and tropical trees,
Of islands lost in the Spanish Main
Which no man ever may find again,
Of fishes and corals under the waves,
And seahorses stabled in great green caves.

Sea Shell, Sea Shell,
Sing of the things you know so well.

AMY LOWELL

CAGED BIRD

A free bird leaps
on the back of the wind
and floats downstream
till the current ends
and dips his wing
in the orange sun rays
and dares to claim the sky.

But a bird that stalks
down his narrow cage
can seldom see through
his bars of rage
his wings are clipped and
his feet are tied
so he opens his throat to sing.

The caged bird sings
with a fearful trill
of things unknown
but longed for still
and his tune is heard
on the distant hill
for the caged bird
sings of freedom.

The free bird thinks of another breeze
and the trade winds soft through the sighing trees
and the fat worms waiting on a dawn-bright lawn
and he names the sky his own.

But a caged bird stands on the grave of dreams
his shadow shouts on a nightmare scream
his wings are clipped and his feet are tied
so he opens his throat to sing.

The caged bird sings
with a fearful trill
of things unknown
but longed for still
and his tune is heard
on the distant hill
for the caged bird
sings of freedom.

MAYA ANGELOU

ALL THINGS BRIGHT AND BEAUTIFUL

This lovely poem first appeared in Cecil Frances Alexander's collection Hymns for Little Children, *which she wrote in the mid-nineteenth century, before she was married and had children of her own.*

All things bright and beautiful,
    All creatures great and small,
All things wise and wonderful,
    The Lord God made them all.

Each little flower that opens,
    Each little bird that sings,
He made their glowing colors,
    He made their tiny wings.

The purple-headed mountain,
    The river running by,
The sunset, and the morning,
    That brightens up the sky;

The cold wind in the winter,
    The pleasant summer sun,
The ripe fruits in the garden,
    He made them every one.

The tall trees in the greenwood,
    The meadows where we play,
The rushes by the water
    We gather every day—

He gave us eyes to see them,
    And lips that we might tell,
How great is God almighty,
    Who has made all things well.

CECIL FRANCES ALEXANDER

SWIFT THINGS
ARE BEAUTIFUL

Swift things are beautiful:
Swallows and deer,
And lightning that falls
Bright-veined and clear,
Rivers and meteors,
Wind in the wheat,
The strong-withered horse,
The runner's sure feet.

And slow things are beautiful:
The closing of day,
The pause of the wave
That curves downward to spray,
The ember that crumbles,
The opening flower,
And the ox that moves on
In the quiet of power.

ELIZABETH COATSWORTH

Elizabeth Coatsworth was born in Buffalo, New York. During her childhood she traveled to Europe, Mexico, Egypt, and around the United States. She finally settled in Maine where she wrote splendid poems for adults and children that reflects her great love of the natural world.

Keep a poem in your pocket
and a picture in your head
and you'll never feel lonely
at night when you're in bed.

The little poem will sing to you
the little picture bring to you
a dozen dreams to dance to you
at night when you're in bed.

So—
Keep a picture in your pocket
and a poem in your head
and you'll never feel lonely
at night when you're in bed.

BEATRICE SCHENK DE REGNIERS

INDEX OF POETS

Index of First Lines

Y

ACKNOWLEDGMENTS

Maya Angelou: "Caged Bird" and "Life Doesn't Frighten Me" from *The Complete Collected Poems of Maya Angelou*. Copyright © 1994 by Maya Angelou. Reprinted by permission of Random House, Inc.

W. H. Auden: "Song of the Ogres" from *Collected Poems*, edited by Edward Mendelson. Copyright © 1976 by The Estate of W. H. Auden. Reprinted by permission of Vintage Books, a division of Random House, Inc.

James Berry: "One" by James Berry from *When I Dance* by James Berry, published by Hamish Hamilton Children's Books. Copyright © 1988 by James Berry. Reprinted by permission of James Berry.

Elizabeth Bishop: "Manners" from *The Complete Poems 1927–1979* by Elizabeth Bishop. Copyright © 1979, 1983 by Alice Helen Methfessel. Reprinted by permission of Farrar, Straus & Giroux, Inc.

Charles Causley: "Miller's End" from *Collected Poems*. Copyright © by Charles Causley. Reprinted by permission of David Higham Associates.

Sandra Cisneros: "Good Hot Dogs" from *My Wicked Wicked Ways* by Sandra Cisneros. Copyright © 1987 by Sandra Cisneros. Reprinted by permission of Third Woman Press.

Elizabeth Coatsworth: "Swift Things Are Beautiful" from *Away Goes Sally* by Elizabeth Coatsworth. Copyright © 1934 by Macmillan Publishing Company; copyright renewed © 1962 by Elizabeth Coatsworth Beston. Reprinted by permission of Simon & Schuster Books for Young Readers, an imprint of Simon & Schuster Children's Publishing Division.

E. E. Cummings: "anyone lived in a pretty how town," copyright 1940, © 1968, 1991 by the Trustees for the E. E. Cummings Trust; "who knows if the moon's," copyright 1923, 1925, 1951, 1953, © 1976 by George Firmage; "maggie and milly and molly and may" copyright © 1956, 1984, 1991 by the Trustees for the E. E. Cummings Trust, from *Complete Poems: 1904–1962* by E. E. Cummings, edited by George J. Firmage. Reprinted by permission of Liveright Publishing Corporation.

H. D.: "Pear Tree" from *Collected Poems, 1912–1944*. Copyrigtht © 1982 by The Estate of Hilda Doolittle. Reprinted by permission of New Directions Publishing Corp.

Eleanor Farjeon: "Sisters" and "The Quarrel" from *Over the Garden Wall* by Eleanor Farjeon. Copyright © 1933, 1961 by Eleanor Farjeon. Reprinted by permission of Harold Ober Associates Incorporated. "Waking Up" from *Silver, Sand and Snow* by Eleanor Farjeon. Reprinted by permission of David Higham Associates.

Rachel Field: "A Summer Morning" from *Poems* by Rachel Fields (Macmillan, NY, 1957.) Reprinted by permission of Simon & Schuster Books for Young Readers, an imprint of Simon & Schuster Children's Publishing Division.

Robert Frost: "Stopping by Woods on a Snowy Evening" from *The Poetry of Robert Frost* edited by Edward Connery Lathem. Copyright © 1923 by Robert Frost. Reprinted by permission of Henry Holt and Company, Inc.

Rose Fyleman: "Mice" from *Fifty-One New Nursery Rhymes* by Rose Fyleman. Copyright © 1931, 1932 by Doubleday and Company. Reprinted by permission of Bantam Doubleday Dell.

Virginia Hamilton Adair: "Key Ring" from *Ants on the Melon, A Collection of Poems* by Virginia Hamilton Adair. Copyright © 1996 by Virginia Hamilton Adair. Reprinted by permission of Random House, Inc.

Seamus Heaney: "Blackberry-Picking" and "Followers" from *Poems 1865–1975* by Seamus Heaney. Copyright © 1980 by Seamus Heaney. Reprinted by permission of Farrar, Straus & Giroux, Inc.

Langston Hughes: "April Rain Song," "Aunt Sue's Storys," "Mother to Son," and "Poem (2)" from *Collected Poems* by Langston Hughes. Copyright © 1994 by the Estate of Langston Hughes. Reprinted by permission of Alfred A. Knopf, Inc.

Ted Hughes: "My Brother Bert" from *Meet My Folks* by Ted Hughes. Copyright © 1961, 1973 by Ted Hughes. Reprinted with permission of Simon & Schuster Books for Young Readers, an imprint of Simon & Schuster Children's Publishing Division. "Roger the Dog" by Ted Hughes from *A First Poetry Book* by Ted Hughes published by Oxford University Press. Reprinted by permission of Olwyn Hughes.

Randall Jarrell: "Bats" and "Chipmunk's Day" from *The Complete Poems* by Randall Jarrell. Copyright by Mrs. Randall Jarrell. Reprinted by permission of Farrar, Straus & Giroux, Inc.

Elizabeth Jennings: "The Ugly Child" from *A Spell of Words* by Elizabeth Jennings. Copyright © 1966 by Elizabeth Jennings. Reprinted by permission of David Higham Associates.

Donald Justice: "After-school Practice" and "On the Porch" from the poem "My South" from *The Sunset Maker* by Donald Justice. Copyright © 1987, 1995 by Donald Justice. Reprinted by permission of Donald Justice.

Jackie Kaye: "What Jenny Knows" from *Two's Company* by Jackie Kaye. Copyright © 1992 by Jackie Kaye. Reprinted by permission of Penguin Books Ltd.

Galway Kinnell: "Crying" from *Three Books* by Galway Kinnell. Copyright © 1993 by Galway Kinnell. [Previously published in *Mortal Acts, Mortal Words* (1980)]. Reprinted by permission of Houghton Mifflin Company.

Myra Cohn Livingston: "Coming from Kansas" from *Worlds I Know and Other Poems* by Myra Cohn Livingston. Text copyright © 1985 by Myra Cohn Livingston. Reprinted with permission of Margaret K. McElderry Books, an imprint of Simon & Schuster Children's Publishing Division.

Donna Masini: "Learning to See" from *That Kind of Danger* by Donna Masini. Copyright © 1994 by Donna Masini. Reprinted by permission of Beacon Press.

David McCord: "The Rainbow" and "Books Fall Open" from *Far and Few* by David McCord. Copyright © 1935, 1965, 1966 by David McCord. Reprinted by permission of Little, Brown and Company.

Marianne Moore: "A Jelly-Fish" from *The Complete Poems of Marianne Moore.* Copyright © 1959 by Marianne Moore, © renewed 1987 by Lawrence E. Brinn and Louise Crane, Executors of the Estate of Marianne Moore. Reprinted by permission of Viking Penguin, a division of Penguin Books USA, Inc.

Ogden Nash: "Adventure of Isabel" and "The Tales of Custard the Dragon" from *Verses From 1929 On* by Ogden Nash. Copyright © 1926 by Ogden Nash. Reprinted by permission of Little, Brown and Company.

Alfred Noyes: "Daddy Fell Into the Pond" from *Daddy Fell Into the Pond and Other Poems for Children.* Copyright © 1952 by Sheed & Ward. Reprinted with the permission of Sheed & Ward, 115 East Armour Boulevard, Kansas City, Missouri, 64111.

Michale Ondaatje: "To a Sad Daughter" from *Secular Love.* Copyright © 1984 by Michale Ondaatje. Reprinted by permission of Michael Ondaate.

Jack Prelutsky: "The Pancake Collector" from *The Queen of Eene.* Copyright © 1970, 1978 by Jack Prelutsky. "The Hippopotamus" from *Zoo Doings* by Jack Prelutsky. Copyright © 1983 by Jack Prelutsky. Reprinted by permission of